A NOVELLA BY

TOTE HUGHES

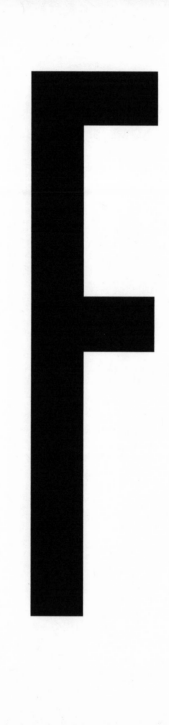

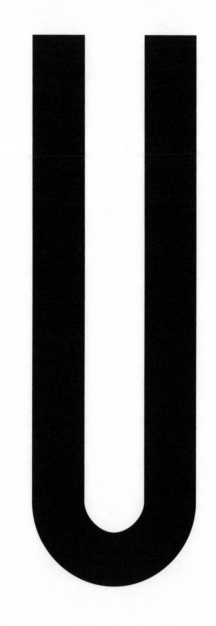

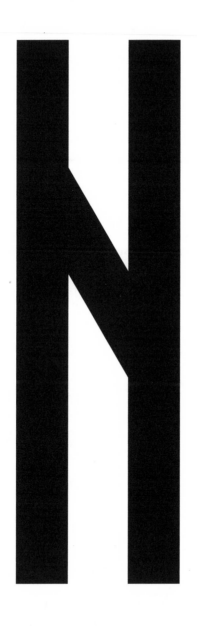

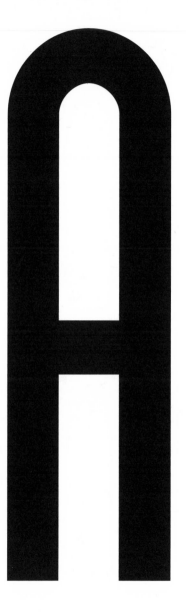

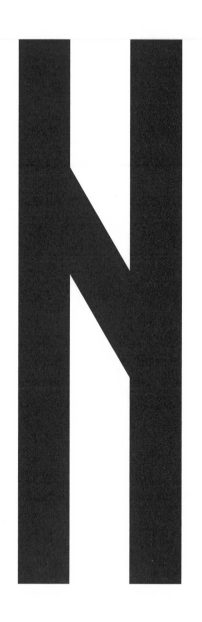

COPYRIGHT © 2014 BY TOTE HUGHES

EDITED BY JOSEPH BATES

EDITORIAL ASSISTANT: SAMANTHA EDMONDS

LIBRARY OF CONGRESS CATALOGING-IN-PUBLICATION DATA

HUGHES, TOTE, 1989–

FOUNTAIN / TOTE HUGHES.

PAGES CM

ISBN 978-1-881163-55-8

I. TITLE.

PS3608.U375F68 2015

813'.6—DC23

2014029930

DESIGNED BY QUEMADURA

PRINTED ON ACID-FREE, RECYCLED PAPER

IN THE UNITED STATES OF AMERICA

MIAMI UNIVERSITY PRESS

356 BACHELOR HALL

MIAMI UNIVERSITY

OXFORD, OHIO 45056

TO W. M. VAUGHAN

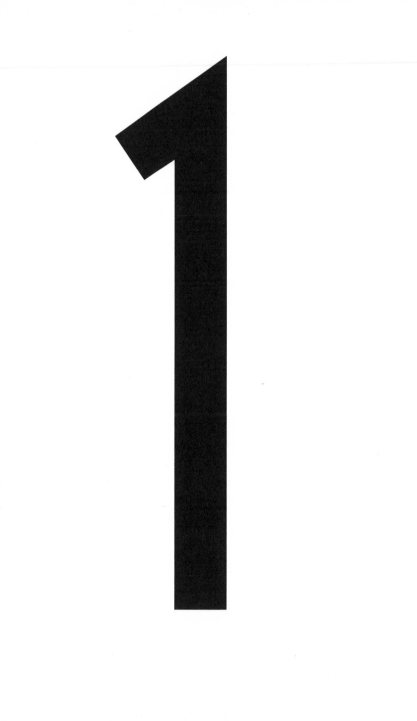

It had become my habit to examine the state of my bed-clothes while dressing in the morning. The condition of my sheets told me much more than I could remember of my nocturnal activity, for I hadn't recalled a dream in over five years. I learned that my sleep held very little relation to my waking life; I often went to bed in a sullen mood—why would I consider sleep in any other?—and woke up unchanged, but my sheets were never so predictable. Some mornings they were still starched and uncreased as if I'd hovered above them the entire night, while on other mornings they were crumpled into a damp ball in the center of my mattress, a configuration which could only have come from something chewing on them for hours. While buttoning my shirt, I would fish around in the folds with my foot and uncover strange articles: unknown keys, tickets to performances I'd never heard of, and foreign coins.

On the morning of my visit to Mr. Selmare's, my sheets formed a long furrow down the center of the bed, and the covers were piled up by my pillow in the shape of a dead sea lion—or, rather, simply a sea lion, for in my opinion sea lions reliably look dead. In the crevice between the bed and the wall I found a torn note, which I reluctantly read, knowing by experience that it wouldn't be optimistic.

Dear Mr. Cormill,

The payment you made with enviable timeliness nonetheless lacked sufficient quantity. Should your circumstances hinder the precipitation of the remainder, and assuming your opinion of jail to be suitably negative, please meet me at Ralfo's Family Foods to discuss alternate options. Flight, though suggestive of romance, is ill-advised.

Sincerely,

Peter Ralfo Sr.

I am not Mr. Cormill, and at that time I knew nothing of the man. My name is Pinson Charfo. I'm tall enough to be considered good-looking, and my hair has been quite intimate with a number of my female acquaintances. I don't have very much money, but I would never skimp on a bill because I have enough foresight to steal what I can't afford. My opinion of Mr. Cormill was therefore pretty low indeed, though, I confess, I was a little envious of his timeliness. I pocketed the note and decided to visit this Ralfo in the afternoon in order to discover how it came to be in my possession, but first I had to turn my mind to other things.

I'd scheduled myself to visit Mr. Selmare in his photograph shop on the city square, and on my way I had to plan ahead for our conversation. Mr. Selmare was something of a hermit, not due to any philosophical persuasion but, rather, to the combination of a dedication to his business and an absolute lack of customers. His shop was a tidy collection of densely packed shelves, each carefully labeled to indicate the nature of the prints it held. Mr. Selmare lived in the back room, which was also the darkroom. I suspected the fumes had a significant influence on the man: his skin was entirely white and his hair the darkest shade of brown. He moved, birdlike, between stationary poses in a way the eye couldn't quite capture. I had to pick my words carefully with Mr. Selmare because he was a dangerous conversationalist, and that morning I wanted to buy a number of disreputable prints from him.

I considered starting with "Hello, Mr. Selmare," but

there was something wrong with it. I tried it out loud and found that I couldn't say "Selmare" very clearly without a lot of practice. I decided to stay clear of his name: "Hello, I would like to buy a number of your disreputable prints." That sounded pretty good. "Which ones?" he would ask. I planned to reply, "The salty ones, sir!" but, after some thought, revised it to, "Do you have any where the subjects are on an airplane wing?" I didn't expect Mr. Selmare to have prints like that, which was fine because I didn't want anything to do with morally questionable photographs in which the subjects were on an airplane wing, but it seemed assertive enough. The truth was that I didn't want anything to do with any disreputable prints in the first place, but I'd promised my pupil's father, in confidence, that I could find him some.

Sarah Beeley, who lived in the apartment below mine, was just returning home as I went out into the street. I saluted her and she reciprocated with her delicate hand. I can't remember if it was I who had invented the salute and she who copied it, or the other way around, but it was a civilian salute, with a lazy tenderness unsuited to discipline. Sarah had, at different times, been one of the girls quite familiar with my hair;

the gesture was very indicative of our relationship. She was pretty and with a family name so ugly that she was literally aching to get married. I often wondered at my chances. The trouble was my work, and perhaps also my existential terror.

"Pin, wait a minute," she said before I went past her. "I've been meaning to ask you something."

I faced her and smiled; it was easy for me to grin when I had something to do afterward.

"Sure. What is it?"

"I want you to go to a party with me." She was looking away to one side, her eyes slightly lowered. "Tomthy's costume party. You weren't going to go, were you?"

"No, I wasn't, for my usual reasons."

"Will you go with me?"

"Of course," I replied. "But you should know that I'll likely make a scene."

"You won't make a scene. People love you."

Sarah took hold of a button on my coat. She worked it in and out of the buttonhole for a time while I uncomfortably looked at her eyebrows instead of her eyes. I'd once looked too closely at her cheeks and found more hair there than I'd wanted to, and then I'd started to notice more hair on other girls' cheeks. There was something very beautiful about Sarah's eyes, and I didn't want to accidentally notice anything weird about them that I would also start to see in others' eyes.

"Regardless, I'm just warning you," I said.

"It's in my nature to blow that off," she said.

"Sarah, have you ever noticed how people don't take care to examine their food? They might find a hair in it occasionally, but it's just chance. I'm not saying I take more care, but at least I acknowledge that I *could* take more care if I cared enough to stop myself from eating misplaced objects."

"Misplaced objects? I know that one-fifth of cashews have a worm inside, though that might only apply in a different country," she replied dreamily.

"I once bit into a sandwich and found a knife inside. The lady at the counter must have misplaced her bread knife inside my sandwich."

I'd told Sarah that anecdote once before, but because she knew that I knew that she knew that I'd told her that story already, it had a special charm this time. We both smiled.

"The point," I continued, "is that I counted eight misplaced objects in the punch last time we went to Tomthy's."

"But you didn't make a scene about it."

"I didn't make a scene about that, no. I didn't tell anyone, and I kept drinking it, a lot of it. But I did make a scene when I encouraged Patrice to slap me."

"You didn't deserve that."

Sarah finally released my button and looked away again. This time she stared out into the street, her eyes going back and forth as they followed the passing cars.

She said, "Patrice is a bitch," and, after a pause, "I wanted to be a diver."

A long silence later, Sarah turned back to me and told me that the party was in a few nights and that she wanted me to go as a wizard. I asked her what she had meant about being a diver—because Patrice hadn't gone to the party as a diver—and she told me that she had wanted to be a diver professionally. I asked how that was relevant, and she told me that I could go as a shaman if I wanted, instead. I asked if I could go as a deer hunter and she said that I couldn't. We parted ways then and I looked back to watch her climb the stairs. Was the name Charfo any better than Beeley? "Sarah Charfo," I thought. Probably better, but it really was a matter of opinion.

The fountain in the town square was overflowing, but the structure wasn't level and the water flowed off just one side. It was a very nice fountain otherwise: in the center of a circular pool, a granite pedestal jutted elegantly upward and held, at its peak, a bronze sculpture of mermaids massaging the feet of a cowled king. Someone had painted something incomprehensible on the side of the pool, but I didn't think it took much away from the beauty. From the most popular angles you wouldn't have even noticed the water leaking out of it. My destination, though, was the least popular angle, and I saw clearly that the water from the leaky fountain ran in a neat little river right under Mr. Selmare's door. I followed it in and sought out its course through the shop. To the right of the door was a long counter; rows of tall shelves lined with yellow file folders occupied the rest of the view. The path of the water turned sharply behind a shelf.

"You're Charfo, Mavil's tutor," Mr. Selmare said from behind his immaculate counter.

I wasn't sure if it was a question or not, but regardless I decided to stick with my plan.

"Hello, I would like to buy a number of your disreputable prints."

I inched farther into the shop, hoping to see where the stream went. After turning past the shelf, it wound by a stepladder and toward a set of stairs against the far wall, disappearing down into the basement.

"Disreputable in whose eyes?" Mr. Selmare replied, a sneer tearing across his pallor.

"The salty ones, sir," I answered absentmindedly.

I noticed small barriers of crumpled paper along the edges of the water; in many places, they prevented the bottoms of shelves from getting wet. Had someone put the paper there deliberately? If so, why hadn't they chosen a more robust material?

Eventually the silence caught up to me, and I became aware of Mr. Selmare's confused face.

"I'm sorry. I was distracted by this water," I apologized.

Mr. Selmare smiled and emitted something like a laugh but more like a wheeze.

He then replied, "Your answer to my question could have made sense, so I was thinking about how to reply to it logically. I wondered to myself, 'Whose eyes are the most salty?' I thought maybe you were referring to people who'd recently cried or had just woken up. But there were so many other feasible answers: people who had just been in a very windy place, or had been swimming in the sea, or had been staring at the sun. And then, perhaps, there are people who put salt in their eyes for fun."

I realized, at that moment, that I wasn't being assertive enough, and that at the current conversational heading I would end up with a set of prints far more reputable than those I'd promised my employer. I determined that it was best to derail the conversation and to get a new start later on down the line.

"Why do you have water running into your shop?" I interrupted.

Mr. Selmare seemed displeased by the question but came around the counter.

"It's the fountain out there." He pointed through the window in the door. "It leaks, as you can see."

"But why do you let the water run through your shop?"

"Because I can't make it stop."

"You could complain to the city council."

Mr. Selmare rolled his eyes and went back behind the

counter. He began to organize a pile of photographs but stopped when he realized that I was still expecting an answer.

"Charfo, the city would just shut off the fountain. They don't have any money to fix anything."

"Has something clogged the drain?" I offered.

"What drain? It's a modern fountain."

I realized that I had very little knowledge concerning the workings of fountains and only a vague notion of the distinction between a modern one and the sort that had come before. My ploy had worked, though, and I was ready to start in again on the important business.

"About those disreputable prints: I'm looking for a set in which the subjects are flying through the air on the wing of an airplane while engaged in their acts, as it were."

"Their acts?"

"I'm looking for pornographic prints," I insisted. "I would like the subjects to be having sex on an airplane."

Mr. Selmare jumped back and raised a hand to his heart. I waited for him to reply, but he appeared to be too shocked.

"Charfo, what do you think I am?" he finally asked.

"I think you're the man who runs this photograph shop," I replied. "This is a photograph shop, is it not?"

"I'm an honorable man, that's what." He sounded like he was growing very angry, but his face still remained stark white. "And what are you? A lout! Most likely a lout!"

"Ad hominem," I complained, but he kept on going.

"Your poor father . . . I'd tell him, I would. The poor man . . . But I'm glad he's not around to see you buying pornography. I'll report this to your employer. And to the city council!"

He had raised his voice, and his hands were waving wildly but completely unnaturally, as if they were embarrassed in some way. He was performing, it seemed. As far as I knew, he'd never met my father, who spent his days in a bureaucratic office. Furthermore, my father likely had no disparaging things to say regarding pornography, for my mother died many years ago.

"Don't ever step in this shop again. I ban you! I'll write up the notice now: 'By order of Mr. Selmare, the proprietor, Charfo, Pinson is hereby BANNED from Mr. Selmare's Photograph Shop.'"

He'd taken up a pen and was scribbling wildly across

the faces of the photographs he'd organized earlier, but the words were illegible. The point of the pen continued off the prints and onto the counter. The man's extreme movements propelled ink in every direction.

"The fine! It will ruin him!" Mr. Selmare exclaimed theatrically.

My assertive attitude was doing nothing in light of recent developments, so I resumed my inspection of the water. While Mr. Selmare continued to rant above me, I bent down and unfolded one of the least sodden crumpled papers. It appeared to be a terrible sort of advertisement.

How will I remember them?

Consider this: A photograph of your whole family dressed as chickens in front of a rustic barn. Sunset. Perhaps the baby as an egg.

For a limited time, Mr. Evesong and Mr. Selmare are teaming up to provide YOU with one-of-a-kind memories.

Mr. Evesong (costumier) and Mr. Selmare (photographer), extraordinaires in their respective fields, bring their services to YOU at unbeatable prices.

Consider this: A photograph of you and your sweetheart
as lion and lioness in the Serengeti. Sunset. Is there a cub
on the way? Mr. Evesong can accommodate that.

Schedule a shoot now!

I folded the paper neatly and put it into my trouser pocket, next to the note I'd found in my bed. I liked to keep things that appealed to me aesthetically; usually I enclosed them in letters to friends. In this ad, I appreciated the use of YOU and wondered if it was intentional that the last *you* was not in uppercase. Mr. Selmare was still ranting, waving his arms around, and the cash register was on the floor; he'd apparently knocked it off the counter in his exaggerated rage. I followed the water over to the set of stairs where the water flowed down into the basement, but no lights were on down there. The sound of the water echoed back to me from the depths, and I imagined a large cave with little blind fish. I began to descend but soon became unnerved by the darkness and turned back.

At the counter Mr. Selmare was mumbling to himself and twirling his forefinger around in one of the pools of ink.

He looked up at me and said, "It was all an act, obviously."

"Obviously. I noticed that early on."

"I never was good at acting."

"I'm not sure the failure was in your acting as much as your impetus."

"But you see, Charfo, I'm a little embarrassed at the moment."

"It's just pornography. We're both old enough to talk about pornography."

"I mean to say . . . It's not the concept. The trouble is, I've sold all that I had."

"That's all right. I actually don't need the subjects to be on an airplane."

"No, Charfo, I mean every single one of my disreputable prints. I've just sold them all to an anonymous buyer. And now what use am I? A photograph shop without disreputable prints. It's embarrassing. I have to wait at least a week before new ones come in."

This unexpected news was a major setback; I knew of no other place to get the material I'd promised to find. I resolved to keep the development from my employer's ears for as long as I could, but already I felt despair climbing my spine. My employer was a man of means and no doubt a member of any number of occult societies rich gentleman were fond of. It wasn't likely that he would kill me, but he might seriously disturb my well-being. And recently I'd been particularly susceptible to stress. When I'd discussed the phenomenon with my friend Ret Sharing a few nights before, he suggested it might be the moisture in the air. I didn't give this theory much approval—as a man who hobbied electricity, Ret often put too much emphasis on damp air—but I did wonder if the cause was something like air. Maybe something that I depended on and took for granted was failing in some way, and my mind just hadn't recognized it yet.

Mr. Selmare asked if I might, on the off chance, want something respectable. I asked him if there were actually people who bought respectable photographs, and he admitted that he'd never heard of anyone like that, though he didn't see why there might not be some exception out there.

"You really have nothing left? No dregs?" I asked.

"I'm sorry. I have a series of very nice skyscrapers. I'll sell them to you at a reduced price."

"What would I do with a set of skyscraper pictures?"

"You're an imaginative man. I know that. I read your column, you know, though your speaking voice is really very different from your written one."

"It seems ridiculous to me that I should use my creativity to come up with a reason to buy something I don't want."

"Consider this: you're trying to sleep, but you're sick of this dull place. Who sleeps in dull places? Not you, Charfo. You sleep where there are skyscrapers! You take from your bedside table this particular set of high resolution prints and arrange them in front of your drowsy face." He paused. "You sleep on your side?"

"Naturally, my lungs," I admitted.

"You arrange them in front of your drowsy face," he continued, "in a neat little row. Perhaps balancing them against the edge of your pillow. Tonight you sleep among the skyscrapers."

"Do you really think that will work?"

"The pitch? I guess I believe it has a chance of working."

"No, the idea. Do you really think they won't be too close for my eyes to focus if I lean them up on my pillow?"

The concept actually seemed pretty sound to me, but I didn't want to be an easy sell.

"Charfo, if you're not satisfied, you can bring them back for a refund. Though at the price I'm offering, it shouldn't really matter."

"I don't invest my money without return," I replied, using the line of some irritating person I'd overheard in a bank.

"I'll lend them to you for a trial run, then. But if they work, you have to promise to recommend the strategy in your column."

That sounded like a fair deal to me, though I was hesitant to agree to writing anything positive about reputable prints. In the end, we shook hands and I left the shop with twelve photographs delicately tied up in a small brown paper package that fit nicely in my coat pocket. I still felt the despair in my spine, but I did my best to ignore it as I made my way past the leaky fountain and down the street.

*

Here is how I find a cafe when I want to find a cafe: I begin by asking myself where I am and, after I've answered myself with something reasonably close to the truth, then I ask myself where I want to be. "A cafe," I answer. "No, you pedant, where do you want to be after the cafe?" I counter. I then engage in more pedantry because it's important to criticize oneself—"I want to be in lots of different places. Where do I want to be *when?*"— but eventually I make peace and come up with something simple and easy. Sometimes, for example, it's as simple as wanting to be where I am. Then I sit down with myself and look at the city from above and pick a route from where I am to where I want to be. I make sure my laces are tied and set out on the route. If the minute hand of the first clock I see reads an even number, I turn into the first cafe on my left, else I go into the next one on the right.

The cafe I found this morning—shortly after 12:07— was superbly ugly, but crowded, which appealed to me. It was ugly because someone had decided to decorate it with floral patterns in pastel and with lights that were bright enough to discourage eating. I planned to get a few slices of toast and collect my thoughts before going to Ralfo's. The waitress sat me at a small table near the kitchen, and I didn't have the instantaneous courage to tell her I'd rather sit across the room by the window. The chair was cold because it was metal—a stupid sort of chair—and I decided not to lean against the back.

If my nature had been less fevered these past weeks, my topical obsessions and misplaced enthusiasm more tempered, I might have been sitting in a much nicer cafe at precisely this time with Ree Sarli, the dancer. Ree and I had organized the date at a party, and I'd even confirmed it later, but then we met by chance on the street soon after and fell to talking. The night before, I'd been up working on a translation—in fact, the toast I was waiting on was affordable thanks to this assignment—and had become so frustrated that I'd gripped my water glass tightly enough that it exploded in my hand. The next morning, I walked out from the doctor's office onto the sidewalk in front of Ree, who was on her way to a rehearsal. My hand was tightly bandaged, so she naturally asked what had happened, and I told her that I'd thrown my water glass across the room and had cut my hand picking up the pieces.

I could see right away that she was a little afraid of me—a person who throws a water glass across the room and then gets cut on the pieces is a person you don't want to hold hands with—but I carelessly continued, feeling secure because the anecdote was mostly a lie. I

— 22 —

wanted to talk to her about reading, specifically about a mania I'd encountered when reading a really good book which manifested itself as a genuine desire to hurl the book at a wall. My little lie seemed a good tie-in at the time, but the conversation slipped away from me and somehow we were talking about how much I hate theater. She told me that she was late to her rehearsal, and I said that was okay, that we could continue the conversation on the date, which was a dumb thing to say because the conversation we'd been having evidently caused her pain. "Oh," she said, she'd been meaning to tell me that she would have to cancel the date: a last-minute scheduling change from her choreographer. We hadn't spoken since. It was a disappointment, of course, but the event gave me a new impetus. I found that I was now applying myself to distracting tasks that I would have previously procrastinated away due to a fear of aggravating my existential trauma. I considered my quest for the disreputable prints such a task, for though I felt its enigmatic sting, I found myself more and more compelled to pursue its end.

My toast came and I eavesdropped as I ate. Three older women to my right were talking about cigarettes. The one with the brightest eyes, but the least remarkable form, was explaining to the others that she could tell the brand of any cigarette based on the smell of the smoke. Her companions were generally scoffing, but they didn't challenge her to a test of her expertise, a fact I found a little annoying. At another table, a couple was talking hurriedly, their faces close together over the tabletop. There seemed to be an issue with an uncle, and then somehow they were going back and forth asking each other if they really loved one another. Both answered evasively. I wanted to think more about this couple but someone spoke in my ear.

"Pass the ketchup."

At once I decided the man who'd asked was unappealing, and I signaled the waitress for my bill.

Meanwhile, he continued: "You had toast? I wouldn't put ketchup on toast in a million years. Tell me, though, I'm curious, was it good?"

"I didn't put any ketchup on my toast."

"My son, you can't keep the stuff away from him. He gets it from me, you know."

I thought about pointing out that his statement was ambiguous, that I could have understood him to be saying he and his son were big fans of toast, rather than ketchup. Instead, I told him I was late for an appointment.

"I have medical problems, too. Mine're in the gut and the groin."

The waitress brought the bill and I paid.

"It's not a doctor's appointment," I said, standing up. "I'm off to see the mayor."

He was suitably impressed by my lie, and I left before he could inquire further.

*

The street was more crowded than earlier, before I'd gone into the cafe. A crush of perfumed shoppers battled vociferous deliverymen, and I wove my way through until I found myself forced off the sidewalk and into the road by two big men in hardhats. The road was a separate melee of cyclists and motorists, a much deadlier conflict which I managed to brave for half a block until I made my way into a quiet alley.

The city was an awesome place, a density of energy that would have been outlawed had it any definable form. On the docks there were a number of old factories, strictly guarded by policemen to prevent people from entering and hurting themselves on the old machines. I sometimes imagined this same police force trying to cordon off the city, to prevent travelers from coming in and getting cut by the saw blades of the city's streets and poisoned by its inhabitants' corrosive tongues. And this city didn't have skyscrapers. In a city of that sort, the energy must have occupied all three dimensions, and the police would have given up and left to become farmers or would have fallen inescapably into the dynamo.

Following the alleys and residential lanes, I came, by a roundabout way, to Ralfo's Family Foods. It was a hulking structure that occupied the entire block and rose six stories into the air. From any direction, you could see at least one of the smiling corncob logos which jutted out over the street from each of its four corners.

Inside I gave my name and was told by a cashier that I'd have to wait until after lunch to see Peter Ralfo Sr. I wandered up and down the aisles in the meantime and prepared a few things to say. I wanted to find out why the letter had been in my bed that morning, but I didn't, of course, want to tell Ralfo that I'd found it there; that would have given him undesirable impressions of my character. Instead, I decided to say that I'd discovered it in the street and that I was worried Mr. Cormill never received it. I was pretty sure Ralfo wouldn't ask me where exactly I'd come across the note, but I decided to tell him I'd found it by the leaky fountain if the question came up. What really bothered me was how to get more information on Mr. Cormill. He really wasn't my business, and I had no tactics for talking about things that weren't my business other than simply talking about them; this tactic usually failed to be useful. As I strolled past the canned tomatoes, a quiet girl in a Ralfo's uniform came up to me and said that Ralfo was ready to see me. I wondered if her meek aspect was simply her personality or the result of her personality being overshadowed by the overly happy ear of corn painted onto her vest. The employee didn't want to talk and avoided eye contact, so I was relieved when she deposited me in front of a gray office door. She knocked very quietly and then hurried away before Ralfo called for me to enter.

Peter Ralfo Sr. sat behind a wide desk. He was fat and wore a green suit that reflected an unpleasant color onto his face. His dark hair was slicked back and crowned with a cowboy hat which was pitched impractically to one side. He held his hands together in front of himself, clearly resting them on his paunch. Ralfo had a number of rings on his fingers: one was certainly a wedding ring and another was related to the army; the rest were turned to face inward in the spirit of secret societies. Disappointingly, his shoes, propped up on the desk, were shiny and black; I'd expected tall boots. One of his shoes was single-knotted while the other was double, and this carelessness made me wonder that maybe there was no special reason his rings weren't all visible.

In a clear and commanding voice, he said, "Eh, this is Charfo?"

I looked around, though I was already sure no one else was there. Instinct told me to answer, "This is Charfo," but I quickly decided against it.

"Hello, I'm Pinson Charfo. I've come to return a note to you."

I proffered the letter meant for Mr. Cormill, and Ralfo took it carefully and held it up before his face. He took a long time reading it and mouthed along as he did, even the punctuation.

"I found it on the street," I added after a time.

Ralfo soon dropped the paper onto his desk and cleared his throat.

"It's a weird letter," he said, eyes narrowing.

"I was worried that Mr. Cormill never got it, so I thought I'd bring it to you."

Ralfo chuckled and repeated, "It's a weird letter," and then rose from his desk.

He went to a cabinet and prepared drinks, and I looked around. There was only one chair, the one behind Ralfo's broad desk, and the walls were papered in certificates. They didn't seem very prestigious; most were awards for completing various business workshops, but there were a few depicting endangered animals he'd donated to support. There was also a very loving note from Ralfo's mother, which had apparently been sent to him when he was much younger.

"Here," Ralfo replied, handing me something alcoholic.

He walked to his desk and sat on its surface, indicating that I should sit similarly beside him. Without facing one another, our conversation developed a wistful air which lent itself better to being held outside.

"I admire your skill. You're hired."

"What?" I asked.

"I don't usually go for these ploys, but you've got something good. I hired a man once because he brought me a live chicken. That was more interesting than your letter, but you've a better face."

So Ralfo hadn't written the letter. The way he looked and spoke conflicted with the letter's language. He evidently thought I'd written it as a way of impressing him. Was there truth to that? Had I sleepwritten it? I'd never done something like that before, as far as I knew. In any case, I wouldn't have written it to impress him, that much was certain.

"But who's Mr. Cormill?" Ralfo asked me. "Is that a reference to a famous person?"

I decided it was time to confess the truth, to tell him I'd not written the letter and that I was even more confused than him on the subject of Mr. Cormill, but then I changed my mind. I wasn't positive that I wasn't the author, and the idea of unknowingly penning an impressive work appealed to me. There was an anecdote on the edge of my mind that related to this situation, but I couldn't quite recall it at the time. The very existence of this anecdote, though, whatever it was, lent the wistful air a romantic one, and I felt myself compelled to contribute to the mystery at hand.

"Mr. Cormill is a cartoonist. He makes those political cartoons for papers," I lied. "He's in debt, although his salary isn't bad, because he's a womanizer and a gambler."

"A good person to use in your note, then. Good. Well, Charfo," he said, rising, "I need your help with something I've been trying to write."

He took a sheet of paper from his desk and passed it to me. It read as follows.

Dear Carolina,

Deep inside my chest I feel a pain. It feels like it's going to explode. Explode like a stick of dynamite in the ass of a steer. You treated me nasty.

Next time we pass on the sidewalk you look left and I'll look right. That way our eyes won't see each other.

You did an act of treachery when you came to me last. I know you lied to me. Because of your act of treachery I'm going to get mad and set something on fire. I'll let you guess what.

Sincerely,

Peter

I took a breath and looked up. Ralfo was preparing another round of drinks at the cabinet, and I saw that the back of his suit jacket was marred by a dark patch of sweat. He didn't look like I'd imagined an arsonist to look, but did that mean he wasn't really serious, or that I was just naive? Either way, I didn't want to be on his side. If he wanted my assistance with the letter, then I needed to worm something into it that would tell this Carolina to come to me for help. Though I knew nothing of the woman, I prickled with the thought of her delicate hand knocking at my door and the soft accent of her voice detailing her woes. I would offer her a handkerchief to dry her eyes.

In that instant, I realized that I'd really gotten myself into a tricky business. The despair in my spine began to throb, and I wanted desperately to lie down in a corner somewhere. I had no prospects for my disreputable prints, and now I was embroiled in a lovers' quarrel between a fat man with matches and a breathtaking blonde—she was almost certainly a blonde. I thought about running away to another city. It was a silly idea. My despair was abnormal given the objective triviality of my circumstances; I was in no real danger. I knew, then, that I would be up late sorting things out in my mind as I listened to music from the comfort of my bed. I suspected that there was something else, really terrifying, that I hadn't yet become conscious of.

"So, Charfo, cut to the chase. Give it to me raw," Ralfo said, handing me another one of his ugly concoctions.

"It's very good. I've only a few suggestions."

Ralfo took the page from me and sat at his desk. He took up a pen and held it expectantly over the paper.

"First," I began, "you need to add commas. A lot of commas."

I was buying myself time. Ralfo hesitantly put some commas between various words. Whenever he looked up at me, I smiled and nodded.

"Commas are the essence of good writing. Oftentimes a single comma in a sentence will say more than all of the words combined."

I was struggling to figure out a way to put my name into the letter in such a way that Carolina would think to come to me. I wondered if she ever hobbied codes and ciphers. Her name didn't suggest it, but then again, my name was Charfo. Maybe she had a really pretty last name.

"What's Carolina's last name?"

He was still adding commas. "Meesquich."

I put my head in my hands.

"Should I put that in here somewhere?" he asked enthusiastically. "Maybe 'Dearest Meesquich' at the top?"

"Sure," I said.

What was I doing? No one with a delicate hand and a soft accent had a name like Carolina Meesquich. It was a bust, I concluded.

"What else?" came Ralfo's excited voice.

"Emphasize the treachery she committed. Use that word, 'committed.' Go a little more into the details. It'll make her feel worse. Also, be more liberal with uppercase."

It occurred to me that I shouldn't abandon Carolina just because she had a terrible name. She was still Ralfo's enemy, so she couldn't be that bad. The intrigue was what really appealed to me anyway, not Carolina herself, though it would certainly help if she remained a slender blonde. And then, a good idea came to me.

"And put this in: 'Take a look at this morning's paper, the Charfo Column. You'll find a little treat there.'"

Ralfo was genuinely confused.

"I write a column for the paper. On the morning she's to get this note, I'll put a report in my column about a car that was set fire to last night. Or something to that effect."

His eyes began to twinkle. "It'll scare her ass back into the cow!"

The man's fixation with vulgar, livestock-related turns of phrase was confounding. How central was it to his character?

I would, of course, write something very different in my column, something mysterious that would make her come straight to my door. I wasn't sure yet, but maybe it would involve a long-lost sister.

"Well, Charfo," Ralfo cried, taking a leatherbound checkbook from his desk and scribbling in it, "you've been worth every penny!"

"I'm happy to oblige," I said, resisting the urge to immediately look down at the check he handed me.

"I'll sic this randy bull on her in two days' time. So, don't bungle it now."

I promised to write a juicy piece for my column and then escaped into the afternoon. It looked like it was going to rain.

*

Ralfo had given me a surprisingly good amount for my services, so, after spending a couple hours practicing my writing in a cafe, I struck out for my friend Grel Sinders's place in order to take him to dinner. Grel was significantly poorer than myself; I knew it would please him immensely to get a free meal. He could also help with my unfinished pornography problem, I thought, since his elder brother was one of the most unseemly men I'd ever met.

Grel's apartment was high up in a building of terribly odorous cells that were alternately occupied by screaming families and unemployed alcoholics. Grel never complained to me about his lodgings—I sometimes wondered if he'd even move should he come across the cash—but they were objectively dismal. Once, walking up to the building's entrance, I'd heard a number of cries and a whistling in the air, and just as I jumped back, a mattress crashed to the sidewalk and exploded into a shower of screeching rats. I was quickly informed by two unfazed children playing nearby in the pebbles that Mrs. Relfy had discovered the rats inside her mattress a few weeks ago but had only decided to take action today. The night before, the bed had moved back and forth across the room as its restless inhabitants scampered around in search of scraps, and Mrs. Relfy hadn't been able to sleep at all because of the seasickness.

I resolved that day never to go into Grel's apartment building again and to send up one of the readily available urchins to bring Grel down to the street if I needed to talk to him. Of course, he had no telephone.

Striding from the shadow of the wretched interior, Grel beamed and adjusted his scarf. He wore a navy coat from some foreign military and his hair was dark and wild. The coat did an admirable job of hiding the greasiness of his clothes, and his face was cleanshaven and sharp, so that, especially in the dim light of the overcast sky, he looked elegant, if a little artistic.

I turned in the direction of the more moneyed districts, and Grel fell naturally into step beside me. We needed no communication to signal the beginning of a walk; it may have been due to the fact that we had first met while strolling, admittedly not quite soberly.

"I've some news for you, Pin," Grel began after a block. "Bernsy wants to fight you. I think he used the word 'satisfaction,' but then he shouted some pretty unsavory things, ruining the effect. We were in an establishment, you see, so there was general cheering."

"What? I haven't seen him in weeks."

"Bernsy told me, and everyone else in the bar heard it clearly enough, that you stole his work and published it."

"I don't even know where he lives," I objected.

"What's that got to do with it?"

"How would I get his work if I wanted to steal it?"

"There're plenty of ways. A pickpocket simply needs a pocket."

The rain began to fall then, and I pulled up my collar—it was what movies had taught me to do, though it did nothing to protect me from the water.

"Bernsy will be at Tomthy's, won't he?"

"You're going? Of course he's going. That'll be quite the scene. I'm going," he answered.

"I told Sarah I'd cause a scene, and now it's inevitable. Nothing good ever comes from going to Tomthy's."

The conversation languished for the remainder of our walk to the restaurant, but I used the time to think about what to tell Grel of my recent adventures. I decided to keep silent about the Ralfo story, but his brother's help with the prints was going to be invaluable, so I decided to tell him all about that mission. The rain worsened until we were leapfrogging from awning to awning. Grel whistled a tune from an opera about a nuclear submarine. At the door to the restaurant, he protested, citing the price. I used the phrase "my aunt died" to preserve my secrets and Grel, honorably, asked no questions and acquiesced to dine on my bill.

As we waited to be seated, Grel wondered, "What kind of wizard are you going as?"

"I want to go as a deer hunter, but Sarah won't let me," I replied.

"Sarah Beeley, what a name!"

"She said I could be a shaman."

"That's not bad. What kind will she be?"

"You know, she never told me. I didn't think about it until now, but she's got to be up to something. Asking me to be a wizard or a shaman, she's very clever. I might marry her some day."

"Sarah Charfo, what a name!" Grel said.

We were seated then, and Grel quickly tucked the napkin into his shirt to obscure its ragged appearance.

"Grel, we'll come back to the subject of Tomthy's. I need your help with a project."

Grel eagerly nodded. Behind him, a pair of enormous businessmen were drinking liters of wine and talking very loudly about retirement plans. I described my unsuccessful search for the disreputable prints in a hushed voice.

"Let me see the skyscrapers."

I didn't see how it was relevant, but I knew this was how Grel thought. He never went straight at the target but always swerved around and talked deeply about tangents until somehow he inevitably ended up with a real bullseye of an idea. I went to my coat—it was the sort of place that took it at the door—and fetched the prints from the inside pocket. On the way back to the table, I caught the hostess watching me. I smiled at her. She smiled back, but quickly looked down.

"What do you think of art theft?" I asked her.

She was a bit taken aback and quickly surveyed the dining room. Only when I reached my seat did I realize that she'd been looking around to see if any of the paintings were missing. I felt like going back and explaining that it had simply been "an aesthetic comment," but Grel had already ripped open the paper and was carefully inspecting the pictures, laying each one out on the table.

"This one's a duplicate," he announced.

"You can have it."

"Thanks," he replied enthusiastically. Then, after admiring it further, "The way I see it, the tactic's got to work. Did you know that you open your eyes all the time in your sleep? I don't just mean you, I mean everyone."

The fact sounded reasonable to me.

"Grel, what do you think of the problem?"

He thought for a moment.

"Do you think Mavil's father is the kind of man who would make trouble for you if you don't get him what he wants?"

"Possibly. He's a very serious person with very little patience. Due to the coercive properties of his forceful character, I feel like it's my duty to get the prints for him."

"But he's only paying you to teach his daughter."

"I would like someone with a remarkable set of muscles to tell him that for me."

"It's simple, then. After dinner I'll call my brother. He'll know exactly what to do about the photographs."

His confidence was comforting, and we had a lively argument about dishwashing until our food came. Grel stopped me before I could take my first bite.

"I recently read about a culture that finds it vulgar to eat in front of other people. They still get together for meals, since it's more efficient to make food for a group, but when it's time to eat, they all turn their backs toward the inside of the circle. They'd all been sitting in a circle, before, in order to talk as equals while they smoked. When their backs are turned and they're eating, they don't say anything. Not because talking while eating is viewed as rude, but because it only slows down the process, and they're eager to get back to facing the right way round in order to continue their discussion."

"I reject culture," I told him.

"The fact that I used the word shouldn't change your opinion of the idea."

"What's my opinion of the idea?"

"Definitely positive."

"I'm not going to do that in this restaurant."

"Why not? We pay to eat here. You should be allowed to be even more wild in places where you have to pay to eat."

I was going to have enough trouble eating normally as it was; the hostess kept looking my way with a frown. I took a bite in defiance of Grel's judgmental gaze.

This was typical of Grel. He was very fond of eccentric ideas that generally made the participants act foolishly in public. Being his friend, I'd already had many opportunities to reflect on why I so rarely supported his behavior. I wasn't entirely opposed to making a fool of myself—it happened often to me, and not always by accident—but what bothered me was his justification. Grel always prefaced his proposals with some sort of argument, and this, in my opinion, destroyed any charm, for charm generally came from spontaneity and impulsive eagerness.

Grel began to eat sulkily.

I felt compelled to say something to ease the mood. "Do you remember me telling you a story about someone doing something and then not remembering it? It was something about action, memory, forgetfulness . . ."

I had in mind that anecdote which had been on the edge of my thoughts in Ralfo's office, the one I still couldn't remember.

"Yes, about Gary," he answered quickly.

I didn't know a Gary and told him so.

"Gary, the ecclesiastic who drank. But you didn't tell me that one, my brother did."

"No, this anecdote somehow involves a man and a policeman."

At that moment, an enormous dog with matted

brown hair dove beneath our table and set to howling dramatically. I instinctively kicked at it but lost my balance and went sprawling into a neighboring couple. Grel jumped up and held his fork before him as a fencer would his foil. The other diners fell silent, their mouths parted and eyes indecently exposed. The scene remained like that, still, while I righted myself. I had been punctured in the thigh by a butter knife, but it was nothing serious.

"Where did this dog come from?" I asked loudly.

No one answered, yet the dog shouted eagerly from its fortress.

"What's your name, vile thing? I'll make an enemy of you," Grel said.

He was very serious and his eyes twinkled as if they'd teared up.

Dogs have consistently presented a difficult problem for me from the time I was a child. Many of the books I enjoyed back then included a dog in some significant way, often as a companion to the hero or as a helpful acquaintance along the way. Yet, the real dogs I met on the street bowled me over and barked nastily before snapping at my shoes. They deposited feces in my walking paths and covered the comfortable chairs in their adhesive hair. I became very attached to the idea of dogs but rejected strongly their physical manifestation. I hadn't considered dogs in the intervening years, but now, having one thrust upon me in this way, I quickly remembered the revulsion they could induce.

"Just stab it," I said to Grel.

He hesitated but maintained his determined face.

"Get the hell out of our table!" I shouted and threw a salt shaker at the beast.

The dog didn't react but continued its monologue. A guest put a hand on my shoulder and advised calm. Waiters then tried to be useful: two attempted to tug the dog out from its fortification without destroying our meal, and one went so far as to bring a big bone from the kitchen. Unfortunately, the strength of the animal was no match for the delicate men, and the lure was entirely ignored.

"Don't worry, sir," the hostess whispered in my ear. "We won't charge you for the meal."

"Do we get to keep the dog?" I asked sarcastically.

The hostess stared at me blankly.

"I don't steal art," I told her as I took up a pepper shaker and threw it into the fray.

"We'll sort this out soon."

"Want to go to an art gallery some time?"

The question scared her, I think, because she quickly went away. I thought I'd acted rather coolly in front of her. It was a disappointment.

Then, without any apparent motive, the dog went silent and bolted from beneath the table, out through the restaurant's door. Everything was put back together while I went to the restroom to inspect my wound and to clear the debris from my clothes. When I returned, Grel was eating calmly and the other guests were conversing in hushed voices. Thinking it would be an impressive thing, I took my seat without a word and continued my meal, but no one seemed to care how collected I was.

"I wish I'd had the courage to stab it like you told me to," Grel said quite honestly.

Before leaving, Grel used the restaurant's phone to call his brother. They talked for a long time. I waited outside in order to avoid the hostess. It had stopped raining, and the city now lay in the Earth's shadow. Fins of steam rose from the surface of the street and rushed across the sidewalk, befuddling my eyes. A party of pedestrians careened by in the growing darkness, already past a few beers. They seemed enamored with the steam and embraced the fleeting columns grotesquely as they would harlots, had harlots not been banned many years ago. I shuffled around because the benches were still wet and ended up chatting with a valet about cars in order to occupy my time. He was cheerful and more than once told me that he greatly honored his profession although he used to hate it. At first I remained silent on the matter, but after he repeated the comment for the fourth time, I felt compelled to agree that his profession was indeed noble in order to make him move on to more interesting observations. He didn't supply any. The valet was very good at identifying the models of cars, though, and during our conversation I tested him over and over again on those that drove by. I don't know if he was ever wrong because I know nothing about cars, but he was very serious about it and didn't seem to be showing off. At one point, I told him about a problem Mavil's father had with his car—it sometimes started up spontaneously, often in the night, and rattled—but the valet was uninterested. By the time Grel came out, I was sick of the man.

Grel grabbed me by the arm and pulled me down the sidewalk.

"We're going to meet my brother. Think about it," he said, evidently paraphrasing a part of the conversation he'd just had. "If you were assigned to hand out tickets to a fish fry, wouldn't you sneak one or two into your own pocket?"

I was now walking under my own power but didn't see the reason for all the rush.

"Does your brother like fish fries that much?"

"I'd change it from fish fry to something more desirable, but it's the idea that matters. Mr. Selmare must have one or two 'tickets' stashed away for himself, and we're going to find them."

Grel once told me that he was never obliged to answer a question. He made it clear that this wasn't because he wanted to hide anything, but because all words spoken to someone should be seen as gifts, and gifts, as anyone could tell you, were free from obligation. I disagreed on principle, believing simply that questions needed to be answered at all costs. Truthful answers, though, were not part of the deal.

"And the tickets are probably for the best seats in the house," Grel continued.

"Fish fries have assigned seats?"

"Pin, did you really plagiarize Bernsy?" he asked tangentially.

"Of course not. What does he have worth plagiarizing?"

"That's the thing, Pin. He says he's written a manifesto. A good one."

"But Bernsy's basically illiterate. He put a story in front of my eyes last time. The first sentence used 'but' four times and contained a metaphor about the sea."

"This manifesto really kicks. They say a league's already been founded on it."

I was about to ask for details on the manifesto, but Grel suddenly stopped and turned to me.

"Now Pin, two things to remember about my brother: one, his name is pronounced *reed* even though it's spelled r-e-a-t-h, and two, his wife just left him. He's prone to anger, so treat him right in these areas."

*

Four years ago, I'd been sitting under a maple tree with a book when suddenly my view of the page was obscured by a waving hand. A foul fungal scent took up residence in my nostrils, and I became aware of a chartreuse voice.

"Heeeellloooo," it sang. "Can't read now, can you?"

I looked up and flinched. A curdled nose, spotted cheeks, and little pinpricks of eyes overshadowed by a drooping brow occupied my field of vision. The man was very close to my face and he was breathing hard, as if his hand-waving were costing him dearly.

"Hello," I replied curtly.

"You're Pinson Charfo. Charfo for short. I'm Reath." He stopped waving and held out his hand for a shake.

"I prefer Pin. Charfo is not a good name."

Reath momentarily looked over his shoulder while I spoke. It was a relief to be free of his breath, but he still leaned down over me, preventing me from standing.

"It's like this, Charfo," he said, turning back. "My brother's your chum."

"Do you mind letting me up?"

He moved to one side and tried to help me to my feet, but I did my best to ignore his efforts.

"Who was it who said that? The great philosopher Freedmont if I'm not mistaken," Reath commented.

"You're mistaken," I replied.

"He'd been caught in a bush, fallen out of a carriage while on parade with the king. 'Do you mind letting me up?' he asked the bush."

"Freedmont lived in a democratic time," I corrected.

"Right. I believe it was Joansey."

"There never was and never will be a philosopher named Joansey," I said to him.

I was confused about why I was even conversing with Reath. Where had he come from? Which of my friends did he belong to? These were nice questions, but I didn't particularly care to answer them at the moment. Instead, I planned to get out of view and then find a new tree to sit beneath.

In preparation for my hasty departure, I tucked the book into my back pocket. Mrs. Fiss, my landlady, had once said to me, as I walked up the stairs one night, "A good book must always fit in your back pocket." I'd never been completely comfortable with this statement. Certainly there were a lot of good books that were very thick and had no place in my pants, but, nonetheless, I wanted to agree with her. I'd eventually come to the conclusion that she was talking about the quality of a physical book. A thick book could be a good work, but its existence in book form was a failure if it exceeded two hundred and two pages. Volumes made good works into good books. But reference books were a complication. Every time I pocketed a book, my mind inevitably went through this argument and ended up discontented.

"'Disconsolate scab, your money's the pill.' Ah, Joansey had a way with words."

"I don't know who you're referring to," I said and began to walk away.

Reath quickly caught up to my side, breathing heavily.

"Here's another good one he said: 'Fair well abroad, my treacled plum.' Do you think, Charfo, that we could pop that bar there for some moisture?"

"You're free to act as you wish."

"The trouble is, I've come to fetch you. To return to the hospital empty-handed would be a mistake. To return thirst-unquenched would also be a loss."

"The hospital? Who's in the hospital?" I asked, turning to face him.

"My brother. Your chum, Grel." He could see I was worried by this news, so Reath added, "He's alive."

Reath was an irritating man, I concluded. I asked him for the name of the hospital and ran there, somewhere along the way losing him to a bar. I'd kept clear of him since.

We met Reath at the fountain outside of Mr. Selmare's shop. He was sitting on the wall of the pool with his shoes beside him, dangling his bare feet into the water. The clear night sky was a dominating black. The light of the streetlamps made the empty square feel small and intimate.

"The plan is this," Reath said without looking up from his toes. "We'll pop the shop, snatch the goods, truck to Lion Bar, divide the loot, and split. I've worked it out. As informant, Charfo, forty percent, as accomplice and handyman, Grel, twenty percent. As specialist, me, what's left."

"Forty percent," replied Grel quietly. I wasn't sure if he was asking for more of a share or just stating the left-over amount.

"Mr. Selmare lives in his shop," I pointed out.

Reath produced a length of rope and passed it behind his back to Grel, who held it limply. He was trembling, but so was I, due to my damp coat.

"I don't think we need violence. Maybe we can draw him out on some pretext," I said.

"I'm not unused to criminal patterns," Reath replied. "I called the shop six times and got nothing."

"Maybe he was in the bathroom," I suggested.

Grel retched and lunged toward the fountain, spouting vomit into the pool in a delicate arc. I didn't move to help; emesis is a private struggle, embarrassingly revealing. Eyes averted, I examined myself and found the stress to be absent from my spine. The discovery produced a pleasant sensation. To be free of the burden, if only momentarily, was delightful and titillatingly curious. When had it alighted? Grel whimpered something and then broke off to continue spewing into the water. Reath quickly retracted his feet. In the spaces between his toes, I saw the glimmer of coins; he'd been collecting them while speaking to us, a small fortune of wishes dashed. The man spun round and, crouching on the little wall, plucked the coins from his feet, depositing them into one of his socks, one by one. I watched, mesmerized by the grotesque grin on his face, made fiendish by the sharp street light.

Grel came to my side and whispered, "Sorry."

When Reath was finished, he tied up the sock tightly to keep the coins from clinking and tucked it into his shirt. He vacillated between which foot to put the remaining sock on but eventually put it, too, into his shirt and slipped his dripping feet into his shoes.

He looked up and asked, "Ready?"

I looked at Grel, who nodded slowly. He still held the rope, but the end trailed on the wet pavement. Grel and I had discussed illegal activities in the past with considerable enthusiasm, but we'd never perpetrated anything serious together. I'd always assumed he'd just been stealing and forging on his own, but now I was certain he'd never done anything of the sort.

I held up my right hand, forefinger extended. It was meant to signal "ready," but Reath pointed at me and said "Charfo," calling on me like a teacher would. I just nodded. He turned then and crept toward the door of Mr. Selmare's shop, his shoes making an unhealthy squelching sound. We followed at a distance; I was ready to run should Reath decide to do something extreme.

"The water from this fountain runs into the shop," Grel observed in a whisper.

"It runs all the way into the basement," I replied.

I then told him Mr. Selmare's opinion of the leaky fountain while Reath fiddled with the door. I couldn't see what Reath was doing, but it didn't look like he was picking the lock.

"I wonder if he's using it for developing his prints," Grel replied. "It's free water."

"It's possible. Mr. Selmare's tough to crack."

The door swung open; Reath waved us in. As we stepped gingerly over the little river that ran through the door, I saw that Reath was standing in it, carelessly. Inside, he pointed at me and then pointed at the door behind the counter, then to Grel and the door we'd just come through. He held two thumbs up until we both nodded uncertainly then tapped his wrist where a watch would have been and held up ten fingers. I remembered Reath having a watch and I looked at Grel, trying to convey my curiosity about the matter, but he was busy staring down at the water. When I looked back, Reath was creeping away into the darkness of the shelves.

I did my best to perform the duty I'd been silently assigned, but the door behind the counter was locked, and I wasn't able to see any light behind it. I knew the door couldn't lead to Mr. Selmare's darkroom, which was further back in the shop, so it was probably a closet of some sort. Judging by the door's distance from the wall of the neighboring store, it couldn't have been a big room. Turning around, I saw that the counter had been cleared of the prints and ink, and the cash register was back in place. I tried to open it, but I only made a lot of noise. Losing interest, I went back to Grel. He was reading one of the balled-up advertisements by the light coming in through the open door.

"Pin, I don't think Mr. Selmare is as devious as you make him out to be."

He tried to hand me the paper, but I waved it away.

"I've read it. I admit it's trash, but maybe it's Mr. Evesong's. Maybe Mr. Selmare's using it as a sandbag because he recognizes its deficiencies. There's still room in the scenario for Mr. Selmare to be devious."

"I'm going to save this, I think," Grel replied, carefully putting the page into his pocket.

I didn't tell him I'd done the same thing.

We stood there, looking out into the square. The bronze king on the fountain stood in profile from our angle, and it reminded me of how Sarah looked whenever she pulled her scarf up over her head like a hood. She'd been like that when I first met her, when she'd introduced herself as Dr. Cashmere. Naturally, we'd been much younger. I decided, then, that Sarah would have also kept one of the advertisements, had she been in the shop. I wondered what she could want from me going to the party as a wizard. Did she know about this Bernsy business? I concocted the following theory to amuse myself as I peered out into the night: Bernsy really was illiterate. He hired Sarah to make a copy of a manifesto she'd found in my room, something very eloquent and convincing I'd penned in my sleep. Sarah obliged him, but, shrouding herself in a scarf as she sat at her desk, she made a few alterations. For example, the manifesto said something like, "We are, all of us, workers at heart who strive not for labor, but for recognition," and she changed it to, "We are, all of us, wizards at heart who strive not for magic, but for inebriation." Bernsy, unable to read, spread it about as his work and also secretly submitted it to some publishing houses under my name, one of which had published it. He then started accusing me of plagiarism. Bernsy had done it all because I'd stolen his favorite toy in grade school. I had indeed stolen his favorite toy in grade school, a figurine of a character from Grenswopp, that game people play in cafes. I'd displayed it prominently on one of my shelves for some time.

"Pin, we're going to get spotted as long as we're in the doorway."

Reath hadn't come back, and I was sure that more

than ten minutes had elapsed. I, too, was ready to move on to something more interesting. Motioning for Grel to follow, I showed him to the stairs that led into the basement and pointed down into the gloom. The trickling sound of the water running down the steps appealed to me, and I shivered as if I felt it running down my back.

"I'm going to taste this water," I told Grel.

He didn't answer but took out a lighter and cautiously descended the stairs.

The fountain water tasted fresh, if a little salty, and was invigoratingly cold. As a student, I'd traveled around a little and had made a point of licking all of the important monuments I'd visited. My traveling companions had discussed my project as they eagerly pressed their eyes to the viewfinders of their cameras: it was latent immaturity, it was romantic frustration, it was a protest against consumerism. But they never expressed what I felt to be the real reason: my licking was the ultimate show of respect, the most primal demonstration of appreciation. Drinking this water, I supposed as I knelt there, was something similar. When I'd finished slurping from the stream, Grel was gone; only a faint orange glow emanated from darkness.

I made my way down after him, careful not to slip.

Ahead, I could see the bouncing light of Grel's flame on the walls but, beyond, nothing. When I was halfway down, clutching tightly to the rotting handrail, the light dropped. I could see that the lighter was lying on dry ground; Grel's shadow cavorted around above it in a frantic circuit, but I wasn't able to make out anything distinct.

"What do you see?" I whispered from above.

Grel didn't answer; instead, I heard the sound of him exerting himself, as if he were lifting things and moving them around. The image of the blind fish in the vast cavern came back to me, and I imagined Grel as a stevedore, moving crates of pale, wriggling animals at a midnight shore. Finally, I came to the bottom of the staircase, and at the same moment, the flame went out. Grel cursed. His voice echoed far away in the expansive blackness.

"There's a boat down here," Grel whispered. "I just accidentally kicked my lighter into the water. The whole basement's flooded!"

"A boat?"

I felt around with my foot and found where the steps ran into the water; even through my boot, I could tell it was frigid and still. I dipped my hands into the subterranean lake, and when I pulled them out I didn't feel them resurface. I had to bring my numb fingers to my face to convince myself they were still attached. I repeated the procedure, dunking my hands over and over, marveling at the sensation.

"I think I've untied it," Grel said. "Where are you? I'm going to climb in."

"I'm right here. Put your hands in the water. Without seeing your hands you don't even feel them."

I heard splashing to my right and a cry of astonishment.

"It's amazing, right?"

"Damn, this water's cold! I'm wet to my knees. A part of this step's missing," Grel replied.

I inched toward his voice. There was more splashing.

"I'm in the boat," he said. "Come here, but don't step there."

I stepped there and slipped. The sensation I'd felt in my hands overwhelmed my entire body and my eyes exploded in white flashes. I was floating, flying through a blizzard above an arctic world. I tried to brush the snowflakes from my eyes, but more came and my sluggish hand was ineffective. In desperation, I kicked with my feet and lost my balance in the air, careening through the howling wind into the darkest storm clouds. There was thunder all around, and I saw a flock of sea birds flying by in the other direction. As they passed, they turned to me as if trying to speak, but the wind tore away their words. Trying to regain control, I kicked with my legs again and dove headlong into an ice cliff. I stared wonderingly up into the gray sky as I fell inevitably to my death.

*

Grel was speaking slowly somewhere above me, but I wasn't listening. I was wrapped in a cocoon of thick woolen blankets. Somewhere nearby in the corner of my eyes there was a dim lantern shining. From its lazy swaying, I could tell we were in the boat Grel had discovered. I felt fantastic, warm, sated, and irrational, and I hollered with all of my heart at the black above, my eyes closing and back arching with the effort. In the silence following the reverberation from the invisible bounds of our mysterious domain, I heard Grel's voice droning on indifferently.

"There's a major difference in their style," he was saying. "For example, Remlach is enamored with color.

Even in his dry, technical works, he always manages to include an example which involves colors in some way. Either red and green lights, or blue and red particles, there's always a distinction made with color. Some people say that they think in words while others say that they think in images, which they then translate into words. Remlach might do either, I don't know, but I'm certain whatever he's thinking—whether it's the phrase 'Shading geometry' or some image of the concept—it's in color."

"Grel, why are we in this boat?" I interrupted.

"Oh, Pin?"

"Yes?"

"Wow! You're awake!"

"Didn't you hear my shout?"

"You've been shouting off and on for the past whatever. I have no idea how long it's been. Actually, it must have been about two hours. I've been through my lecture four times."

"I've been shouting for hours?"

I had noticed that my voice was husky, but I'd assumed it was just from my most recent shout, or my recent submersion.

"I managed to get you out of the water before you really died, but by then I'd lost track of where the staircase was."

"What?"

"I got you into those blankets and, in the process, found this lantern and a matchbook. There are crackers and canned meats too. This boat really is prepared."

"But you're saying we're lost? Why didn't you follow a wall?"

"I haven't found one yet. That was my first idea. This is one enormous basement. That, or it's one stationary sailboat."

"It's a sailboat?"

"Yes, but there's not much of a breeze."

I decided to stop asking questions at that point. Considering our circumstances, deliverance was not particularly within our control. No one had come to rescue us after two hours of my screaming, and we hadn't come to a wall despite Grel's best efforts, so we might as well lie back and look up into the darkness and wait.

"I hear water dripping somewhere," Grel said softly after a silence during which I might have slept.

I could tell by the sound of his voice that Grel's head was facing upwards. He was lazily chewing on something crispy. Listening to him, I couldn't help but gag at the thought of eating while on my back. When in school, I'd been told by an expert—had it been an astronaut?— that a person didn't need gravity to eat, that the muscles in their esophagus were enough. That night, I smuggled a roll of biscuits into bed with me and choked on the very first one.

"I hear each drop echo four times. Sometimes I even hear a fifth echo," Grel continued; he sounded very tired. "I never hear a sixth."

"Sometimes," I replied, "I play tunes to myself by tapping different parts of my ears."

"I'm at the limit of my senses. I'm straining to the maximum to hear the sixth echo, but it's beyond my perception. There's a satisfaction in trying to get your body to do something it can't, and I'm striving for it. But what if that satisfaction, too, is beyond my perception?"

"Can you equate feelings and senses like that?"

"Am I equating them?"

"I don't know. I can't remember what you just said."

Grel didn't respond but kept chewing, delicately, as if the cracker were perched uncertainly on his lower lip. In the silence, I reflected back on my day and made a few mental notes which I promptly forgot because right then, for no reason other than the lack of external stimuli, the lost anecdote I'd been looking for came welling up from the depths of my memory. I recounted it out loud, compulsively, to fill the gap in our discourse.

"I'm going to share an anecdote with you. It's not about me. It's about a man named Finch. He ran a flower shop downtown. Although he was very good at accidentally killing the flowers he grew in his own garden, his business did quite well thanks to his employees. His favorite was a foreign girl named Sharpay, to whom he would, a week later, meet among the lilies and stammeringly confess his love. She would turn Finch down but give him a long kiss and run her fingers through his hair. She would tell him she was married.

"Finch was riding a train one morning from his home to his office. He sat by the window on the right side because he looked forward to passing under the Hellisponding Expressway and seeing the pilings that supported the roadway all line up to create the illusion of an endless, luminous tunnel. When he heard the sound of the conductor's ticket punch from the neighboring car, he reached into his coat pocket to take his train pass from his wallet. Finch never displayed the pass before he heard the conductor, because he didn't want to risk someone running down the car and snatching it from his seat. This morning, though, the wallet he found in his pocket wasn't his. It was brown and new. The polished shine hadn't yet been rubbed off by use.

"After checking his pockets a second time and finding no other wallet, Finch hesitantly opened this unfamiliar one. Inside was everything you would expect: a bicycle license, a library card, two old photos, a couple of bills and stamps, a bank card, and, just where he himself kept it, a rail pass."

I paused and sighed. It was an effort to tell this anecdote because my voice was very hoarse. I opened my eyes and took off one of the blankets; it was getting warm.

"I'm listening," Grel said.

"I know, I just had to collect myself," I replied. "It's difficult to tell the anecdote from this point on."

"Do your best."

"If you or I found someone else's wallet in our coat, we would jump right into the spirit of it. First, we would take out our notebook and list all the items in a detailed way. Then, you would claim the pass as yours and hide the wallet beneath your thigh until the conductor was well into the next car, and then get off at the next stop to call a newspaper. On the other hand, I would likely impersonate the wallet's owner, going so far as to introduce myself to the lady sitting beside me. I would get on well with her and I'd give her my address, the one written on the stranger's cyclicense. But, the point is, Finch is a different sort of man. Finch was very worried about where his own wallet was. He put the strange one back in his pocket and searched around frantically. The lady sitting next to him became upset and moved across the aisle—she had been reading a book. Finch was still patting everything down when the conductor came to his seat. He tried to explain the situation but did a poor job of it, and the conductor asked him to get off at the next stop. Staggering from the car, Finch cast his eyes back and forth across the platform, somehow hoping to find his wallet. He was very clearly distressed.

"A policeman, the sort important enough to carry a gun, noticed Finch's despair and offered his help."

"What kind of gun?" Grel interrupted.

"I don't know guns well enough to answer that. A pistol, definitely, but that's all I want to say. In any case, the policeman was much more patient with Finch's stammered explanation than the conductor had been. He asked for the mysterious wallet and then brought Finch down to the station to record all of his information 'in the proper way.'

"The station is the scene of the anecdote's confusion. Right away, the policeman asked Finch for his name. 'Finch Kasto,' he said, offering no spelling. The policeman began to write it down, but then stopped and just stared at Finch, eventually saying, 'Finch Kasto? But that's the name on this cyclicense.' He held up the card from the stranger's wallet beside Finch's face, in order to compare the photo with the man that stood before him. 'This is you,' the policeman said slowly. 'But I don't know that man. The wallet's not mine, nor any of that stuff,' Finch stammered. 'It's your wallet. You're telling me your wallet isn't yours?' 'Look,' said Finch, becoming indignant, 'I know what is and isn't mine.' 'Your name is on every card!' 'It's not my name! It might look like my name, but it's not mine.' 'Frankly, that's nonsense. I'm not going to record that in your statement.' 'You're nonsense!' Finch exclaimed. 'Your helmet looks just like any other policeman's helmet, but is every other policeman's helmet yours?' 'But a name isn't a helmet!' cried the policeman. 'Neither is a rolling pin, yet the same principle applies to rolling pins.' 'I'll concede that. But the coincidence of it . . . ' replied the policeman. 'It is astonishing, but that's the world we've been given,' said Finch, in a victorious tone. The policeman didn't say much after that but kept the mysterious wallet and told Finch that he'd contact him should anything turn up. Finch even managed to get 'compensation' from the policeman, considering the 'inconvenience' he'd gone to in returning the wallet, and then caught the next train.

"The policeman was bothered by the incident and thought about it all day like a reasonable sort of man, the sort allowed to carry a gun in the first place. That night, he convinced himself that the coincidence was technically possible. The next night, he reasoned that anything was technically possible, so where did that leave him? The following night, the policeman decided that Finch was a devious thief. On the fourth night, the policeman came to the conclusion—with the help of his bellicose long-term girlfriend—that it was best to stop thinking about the matter. But, in the end, what kind of reasonable person can resolve to not think about puzzles? Identifying willpower is just another way of defining personality. On the last day of the week, the policeman shook his head for the last time. He liked to think reality was all of the probable possible things that happen. Sure, occasionally a few improbable possible things got mixed in, but that was okay as long as they didn't interfere with law enforcement. That a man should have found in his pocket the wallet of another man with the same name and face, at exactly the same time that he found his own wallet to be missing, was definitely too much of a police-confusing improbability to be accounted real. The policeman took the wallet and mailed it to the Finch Kasto who'd turned it in, the only one he supposed there ever was.

"The next week, Finch received the wallet in the mail alongside a little note from the policeman saying, 'I believe this is yours, we found it on a train.' Finch cried out in delight, for it was exactly his wallet, the one he thought he'd lost forever. And though, for the rest of his life, he commended the police for their skill in tracking down his wallet, he never once realized that it was the very same one he'd turned over to them in a moment of extreme existential forgetfulness."

"I like it," Grel said. "Though I thought it was going to end with the policeman realizing his own name was Finch Kasto."

My voice, by the time I'd finished, was unreliable and on the brink of going away for good. I told Grel that I liked his ending, that I might use it some time, but that my voice was painful, and I wanted only to listen for a while.

Grel replied, "Okay, I'll say some things," but he didn't follow up.

He seemed to be thinking privately. I shuffled off the rest of the blankets. My clothes were still damp, but the air was pleasant, so I stood up carefully and urinated over the side of the boat. The sound was different from the sound the running water had made at the foot of the stairs. The difference came from something external, though, because the fundamental sounds, I realized with a smile, were almost morphologically the same. The sound of my peeing was simply more muffled, more contained.

Grel began, "I don't live in a beautiful place. You know that. But I have tea and a bed, and for the most part I can spend my time out on the balcony that I rigged up."

By the lantern light, I could see Grel reclined in the back of the boat, one hand lazily on the tiller and another near the slack mainsheet. Before, I'd assumed he knew how to sail, but I realized I didn't have any basis for that assumption. The way he sat there, Grel looked like a man who'd fallen from the sky and landed in the back of the boat in generally the right orientation of a nautical man.

"My love interest in this little story is named Drea, a girl by chance," Grel carried on. "At the beginning of the story, we're already well-acquainted. She's allowed to come out on my balcony, and we read together and then start talking once it gets too dark to read. We talk late into the night, sometimes so late that it becomes day again and we resume our reading. One day, the balcony shudders and tilts about twenty degrees downward, but we're able to make it back through the window and into my room before any accident takes us. After that, we tie ropes around our waists and fasten the other ends to the radiator before we venture out. I'm able to convince Drea that it's safe by telling her that I know a lot about sailing and, therefore, knots.

"We talk about all sorts of things, but Drea always likes to bring up the subject of psychic abilities. I find it extremely endearing, though maybe someone less in love with her would find it oppressive. She doesn't directly believe in extrasensory exploration, but it's beautiful to her in some way. Remember, conversations have two fundamental elements: teaching and argument. No matter the relative combination of the two, though, conversations are driven by two entirely different forces: compulsion and decoration. Drea chooses to adorn her conversations with ESP, while others decorate them with dogs, children, dreams, cars, or whatever. It's sometimes a very sticky business, separating out the compulsive dialogue from the ornamental kind, but it's possible to do it if your interlocutors are sane. It might even be that insanity is defined by the point at which a person's idea of beauty coincides entirely with the subject of their instinctive expulsion of words. But everyone has fun defining insanity in different ways. Usually, they like to lay the border in such a way that they sit just safely outside its domain.

"Drea and I go to a park one day by train. It's a nature park, and we bring a backpack of nice food. She's well off, I should add, which is how she can spend all day reading beside me. Would it have been better if I'd phrased that the other way? I'm unemployed, which is how I have the time to spend all day reading beside her. We sit down on the grass in a quiet place."

Grel paused and rummaged around in the dark corner of the boat.

"That reminds me," he said, his head tucked away in a shadow. "There are some q-tips in here."

I welcomed the intermission. Grel's monologue rang strangely in my ears. I'd never heard of Drea; Grel had never mentioned her to me before. Of course, I assumed the worst: she was dead now, and he was probably getting to that with the nature park scene. Drea had been eaten by a bear right in the middle of the picnic, as Grel had been away behind some bush, relieving himself.

"I'm away behind the bushes, relieving myself, when I hear a disturbing noise from under the cottonwood where I'd left Drea sitting," Grel resumed.

He tossed me a q-tip absentmindedly, already working away at his own ear with one.

"It's a polyphonic cackle. Sinister, certainly, but uncomfortably familiar, too. Naturally, in an instant, the flow ceases, and I dash back to the tree. Drea, her back to the trunk, is surrounded by a gibbering horde of ragged people. They're all laughing at once and pointing to something on the ground before her. I can't see what it is until I get closer.

"These people are a mystery to me even now. They wear wild, colorful clothes jumbled together from scraps of found objects. Their shirts are a patchwork of political banners, museum pamphlets, and beach umbrella upholstery. They wear caps, too, from gasoline cans or hubcaps. No unifying symbol is present in their appearance, but these people connect themselves to one another with long nylon cords—maybe it's kite string—which they're always twirling around their fingers. As they career about, like a disoriented school of fish, they pass some custom drink back and forth, taking swigs from either side of their mouth but never the front. It's not uncommon for them to pass the drink by sliding it along a cord by the handle, like a zipline. They haunt me. Not like nightmares, I mean physically. They get into my room, no matter how well I barricade, and, squealing and stomping, they empty my tealeaves onto the floor and transfenestrate my possessions. Tripping against one another in a tangled mass, they always manage to escape before I can hit them in any serious way."

Grel's q-tip jutted horizontally from his ear; his hands were occupied with a packet of crackers.

"I call to Drea, over the jingling headgear of her antagonists, and she shouts back, 'I love you!' Fighting my way through the throng of limbs and string, I'm finally close enough to see the source of their gesticulating. A rough cardboard sign is planted in the ground, facing Drea. Scrawled in black paint, it reads *Does Drea Nordrigal exist?* It's ridiculous, nonsensical; she's there before our eyes. Of course she exists—as much as anything exists. 'Of course she exists!' I shout over and over again as I stumble toward her. 'That's Drea!' I cry, pointing at her. The horde doesn't pay me any attention, so I pull at their arms and hair, forcing them to look at me. 'That's Drea, right there,' I say. They offer me their drink but I knock the mugs away. 'Grel,' Drea whispers, 'help me,' and she collapses to the grass in a faint. I embrace her and lift her limp body onto my shoulder. As I pass, I uproot the sign and wield it like a machete to cut a path through the crowd. They scream when I slice through their nylon connections.

"I carry Drea all the way home, and we recuperate on the balcony. That evening, after contacting the police and discussing the incident for hours, she kisses me goodbye and whispers in my ear, 'See? I do exist.' Now, when I tell her about the hauntings, she insists that the people have never again accosted her, that she hasn't seen them since the park. I've resolved to catch a few of these people for Drea."

Grel smiled at me. In the shadows of the lantern the smile looked sideways. The q-tip was still in his ear, too, which recalled the memory of a girl I'd once met who'd suddenly been distracted after putting eyeliner on only one eyelid.

"You left the q-tip in."

"I know," he replied. "It feels good."

"How come I've never met Drea?" I asked.

Grel groaned and shifted around in the back of the boat but didn't say anything. I had trouble interpreting this answer, so I decided his reaction meant he'd made up the story and was exasperated at me for not understanding that fact. It was probably an allegory for something, which was disappointing, I thought, because I certainly liked the strange people more than the unknown concept they represented.

Suddenly, our circumstances were brought back to the forefront of our minds by a jolt as our boat ran aground on something. Grel held up the lantern to survey the scene. For the most part, the light reflected uselessly off the surface, but after looking closely, we could see some sort of surface just beneath the water. It had a jagged and curiously spotty form and undulated gently in an unseen tide.

*

"We've hit a swamp!" Grel announced.

I dipped a hand in the water; it was much warmer at this spot in the lake. As I felt around under it, I worried for a moment that we were in the same place where I'd peed. It didn't make sense, of course, because pee doesn't keep water warm for that long, but I still felt a little uncomfortable. The underwater surface was made from paper, photographs, I soon realized, as I pulled one out and into the lantern light. The photo I held showed the faces of two children, glaring at the camera, one with a little fist clenched to his ear. On the back, someone had written *Clothus & Monopo, March*. I convinced myself that the writing was Mr. Selmare's. At first glance, the children had just looked like little brats, but turning the photo over again, I realized that they were street urchins. The one with the fist was hiding a deformity of some kind.

"Which one's Monopo?" I asked Grel.

"Look at this," Grel replied, holding up a photograph of a fallen clock tower. "It says, 'The hands still turn!' Does that mean they turn if you push them, or that the clock still runs?"

"Probably the former, but maybe it's an allusion to something."

I took the lantern from Grel and then carefully climbed out into the strange wetland. Though I sank up to my knees, I was still able to move forward. At the distant edges of the lantern light, I saw dark mounds rising from the water. I thought about shouting, "Land ahoy!" but couldn't bring myself to. It was Grel's presence, I think; I'm sure I would have been able to shout it if I'd been alone.

"Are you coming?" I asked Grel.

I didn't wait for an answer and strove onward.

"Yes, but what if there're sharp things under the prints? Like the edges of shelves or rusty nails?"

He struggled to get out of the boat while holding the ball of my woolen blankets above his head.

The dark mounds turned out to be massive piles of photographs, and by the time I'd reached them, I was walking above water level. Unlike the loose prints from where we'd come, the photographs here were bound into nice packets, which formed natural steps up the sides of the photograph hills. Every so often, I saw a distant glow slide into view between the mounds, and I did my best to wind my way in its direction. Grel followed behind me, the bundle above his head bobbing monstrously.

When I wasn't looking for the distant glow, my eyes impulsively scanned the pictures on the ground. I didn't see the photos in their entirety; my eyes only caught glimpses of the images as they rapidly shot back and forth, overwhelmed by the details. Faces of every kind stared back at me from between storefronts and monuments which formed miniature cities beneath my feet. A lion pounced from a great height onto a helpless automobile carrying ice cream bars to a museum. It crashed, of course, and deposited a tire onto a tree. Soon a child was swinging from the tire out over a street where, far below, a dark shadow held a knife to a woman in a glittering dress. I tried to focus my eyes on a single image, but just before I could, they jumped wildly to something else. Behind their frenetic activity, I calmly recalled the time we'd batted a ball far into a field and lost it, and someone had proposed a reward to the person who could find it first. My eyes had wildly scoured the field for hours and even that evening, on the way home, I couldn't keep my eyes from looking for the ball in impossible places: beneath sewer grates and behind neighbors' windows.

Among the photographs, my vision followed a path through a forest, tripping over discarded factories, and came to a crossroad where a couple conversed near an overturned perambulator. Beneath a sign reading *Sefting Cormill, December*, a dark monkey was picking up a crushed skull. Instantly, my eyes jumped back to the sign. I stopped. It was, in fact, a small packet of prints labeled *Sefting Cormill, December* resting against my foot. I picked it up and ripped it open. It held sixteen photographs of a tall man in different foreign places.

"Who's that?" Grel asked over my shoulder.

The light wasn't strong enough for me to look at the photos carefully, but I knew I hadn't seen the man before. The note I'd found in my bed that morning was addressed to Mr. Cormill. I didn't know a Cormill, so if I'd written that note, I would have made up the name. Was this a big coincidence, then? Or, maybe I read the name somewhere and recalled it in my sleep. Or, I could have easily not written the note, I admitted. In any case, I didn't want to tell Grel the truth because it was related to Ralfo, and I didn't want to share that adventure with him yet.

"This guy looks a little like my cousin," I lied and slipped the packet into my coat pocket.

We walked together for a time across the photographs. Soon the glow was visible no matter the configuration of hills. Not long after, we could see that the source was an old-fashioned streetlight standing among the photographs at an extravagant angle. The glow never reached the ceiling of the basement, giving the light the impression of being outside in a wild sort of park. In the secret confines of my coat pockets I ran my thumbs rapidly over the corners of my two packets of prints. I was impatient to look through the Cormill portraits in order to find a clue, but on the other hand, I was exhausted and my drooping lids begged to close in front of the majestic skyscrapers. Maybe when I got to my bed—if I got to my bed—I'd arrange Cormills between the buildings and leave the investigating to my sleepself.

When we reached the streetlight, Grel sat down on his bundle of blankets and opened a bag of crackers. Between mouthfuls, he theorized about the underground world. I was desperately tired and knelt on the ground without listening to him. The air was warm and humid, and I sluggishly positioned my forehead to rest on the cool metal pole of the streetlight. After a minute, I dozed off. I wish I could remember what I dreamt about.

Grel roused me with a rough shake. I was snuggled

into a drift of photographs, my head on a bundle of zoo snapshots.

"Pin! Come on! I found the way out. I followed the electrical cables by digging beneath these prints. They lead to a wall with a door in it and up into one of the old guardhouses on Tisholong Bridge. We've come nearly halfway across the city. It's daybreak out there. We've been down here all night."

I didn't think that was possible and said so groggily.

In his dismissive way, Grel replied, "Let's not debate the nature of time."

I groaned but dug out from my nest. Feeling dehydrated, I struggled with my pockets until they released my sunglasses. As I put them on, the world around me became dark orange and exceedingly difficult to see. Adhering to habit, I kicked around in my bed of photographs but didn't find anything noteworthy. Finally, I leaned against the streetlight and signaled reluctant readiness to Grel with a lazy hand motion. I waited lethargically while Grel organized his bundle of blankets; it seemed he'd wrapped up everything useful he could find in the boat, including, I think, a set of maritime signal flags.

Once on the bridge we parted ways through the waking city; Grel lived to the west and I to the east. I told him I'd come by in the evening to take him to dinner, as the check from Ralfo was still not spent, thanks to the canine. I then stumbled home in my sunglasses, past the people on their way to their business. Mrs. Fiss was already out on the stoop, reclined beneath an upturned bottle of something pungent.

"Good morning, Mrs. Fiss," I said.

For a reason I've always meant to reflect on more deeply, Mrs. Fiss was the only one of my regular acquaintances I greeted with words. She was a big woman, but not fat, with a wooden leg, swollen lips, and an irregular ball of unkempt red hair. She dressed well but never ventured beyond the stoop because everything she needed seemed to come to her. She sorted our mail there, handing it to us as we came by, and fended off the oily solicitors with an old wartime bayonet. On the stoop, Mrs. Fiss was often in the company of a number of well-dressed amputees who cheerfully circulated bottles of alcohol and conversed in monologues. It was common for Mrs. Fiss to occupy a past-due tenant's bed until they paid their rent, and, while it was possible in such circumstances, I've heard, to wedge oneself in beside her, contact with the woman throughout the night would result in waking fully inebriated.

"The Pin returns," she replied after an extended swig. "You had visitors last night: Sarah asked me to give this parcel to you, and a Mr. Cormill stopped by but left nothing except disappointed sighing."

Sarah's parcel contained a wizard costume and a short note saying that the party was two nights away, which meant, I calculated with effort, that it was tomorrow night. I could tell I wouldn't like the costume and decided to find a better one after I slept.

I took the packet of Cormill photos out of my pocket and held one print up to Mrs. Fiss. "Did Mr. Cormill look like this?"

"Yes, that's the Mr. Cormill," she confirmed. "He spoke very well. He's obviously a man of education like yourself. If only he'd had a pegleg, then we'd have had a night, I'm sure. Oh, and you had a strange crew stop by to see you, too. A group of colorful junkyard types who came by to get some books signed."

Immediately my spine tensed once again.

"Mrs. Fiss, did the colorful people have nylon connections?"

"The Pin speaks above my level."

"Were they tied together by string, these people in search of my signature?"

"Yes, they were. They kept getting tangled up. We swapped drinks and talked for some time. They left when Mr. Katto tripped coming by them on the stairs and heatedly hurled one of them into the street."

"They didn't fight back?" I asked.

"I think they wanted to, but they were all pulled down by the strings and couldn't get up for a long time. Here's a bottle of their stuff. They said it was for you, with compliments."

Mrs. Fiss handed me a milk bottle of a liquid I couldn't make out through my sunglasses.

"Last words?" I asked. It was my usual way of saying goodbye to her.

"You're a good boy. Marry Sarah one of these days. And make sure to sleep on your back if you wear those glasses to bed."

I didn't wear the sunglasses to bed because I had to sleep on my side to see the skyscrapers. I pulled the window shades down tight and set the photographs up against my pillow, making a little ridge with my sheets to keep them from sliding around. Carefully, I populated the streets with Cormills. He was a scrawny, dark-skinned man with jagged white hair. Beneath a pair of circular spectacles, he wore a grave expression and a thick brown suit. In his left hand he always carried a polka-dotted suitcase. I was too tired to examine the prints in more detail, but they seemed strikingly similar to one another; the only thing differing between them was the foreign location in which Mr. Cormill stood.

Before falling asleep, I hazily realized that both packets of photographs had been bound in bright yellow nylon cord.

Returning to my bed from the bathroom after a deep sleep, I saw quite clearly from my blankets that I'd been out for some time. They still held my sleeping form, and when I felt around in them for anything interesting, I found them to be warm and humid. I shivered, unclothed, and gripped my hair as a momentary wave of unspecific enthusiasm swept between my ears. I'd heard about this sort of thing from an anecdote, but never before had I genuinely experienced it. My fingers felt every strand, and it dawned on me that my left eye was still closed. I swayed as my vision sparkled. I felt thoroughly confused, mostly about whether or not I was still asleep. I ignored the problem by dropping to the floor to do a series of push-ups. When I returned to my feet, both of my eyes were open, and my veins pulsed pleasantly.

The prints of the skyscrapers were strewn throughout my bedding. A few of them were crumpled up and damp, leading me to believe that I'd squeezed them tightly while I slept. The Cormills, on the other hand, were missing entirely; I spent a few minutes digging around in every possible corner of my bed until I was sure of the fact. I contemplated examining the little windows of the skyscrapers for his recognizable suitcase but stopped myself before following through. It was a silly idea, certainly. The clock indicated that the day had already advanced into the afternoon, and I still had to write my column for the next morning's paper. I dressed, secured some toast, and sat down at my desk.

I've been busy these past few weeks organizing a new kind of club throughout the country. It seems, as a general result of the advancement of civilization, that we rarely recognize we're significantly engaged in battle throughout our entire lives. I've invented the Goose Club to make us aware of this battle and to prepare us for its more dangerous episodes. Well, certainly, you might object. That inasmuch as battle may be considered conflict, we actually do recognize a lot of it every day. But, no, let's think more deeply about battle in this sentence and the little space here—

—for we
want to get at its essence before I describe the details of my recent work: battle is the physical result of pitting two sides against one another, and the more enthusiastically opposed the sides, the more enthusiastic the battle we have.

So, being human, we take the side of humanity and then search, most enthused, for our opposition. What we find, you see, is nature.

Now, why would we want to do battle with nature? It would be easy to say it's simply something in our characters, but one rarely gets anywhere fun by taking the easy route. Instead, let me make it clear that it isn't that we want to do battle with nature, but that we're already doing battle with it. I've constructed the following argument in favor of this proposition:

1. *As young people, we're frightened of dogs.*

2. *What we've once feared, we will forever fear until that fear is maximized or minimized.*

3. *There is no maximum fear instilled by dogs; given a quantity of dog-fear, we may always add to it more dog-fear by simply imagining bigger dogs barking in front of our faces.*

4. *There is no minimum fear instilled by dogs; given a quantity of dog-fear, we may always reduce it by imagining a cuter dog chasing its tail.*

5. *We will therefore never be able to overcome our fear of dogs.*

6. *What we fear, we oppose in equal measure.*

7. *By definition, when we are physically confronted with opposition, we engage it in battle.*

8. *We are therefore in an eternal battle with dogs, though the enthusiasm of the battle may vary significantly across different periods in our life.*

9. *Dogs politically represent nature.*

10. *We are therefore in an eternal battle with nature.*

Whether or not this argument is convincing is likely a matter of schooling. Once you get it, though, you will understand why it's necessary to enroll in a local Goose Club. You see, suppose you're confronted with a particularly bad day of nature-battle. Without preparation you might be overwhelmed and routed. But—attention, now—how can you lose a battle that you must engage in every day of your life?

Logically speaking, you must die. And so, naturally, we want to prevent that.

A Goose Club operates in the following way: members are directed to wait in the attic of the clubhouse while angry geese are introduced through doors on the ground floor. Members are then asked to make their way outside. Battle ensues and experience is gained. You might wonder why I have not chosen to invent Dog Clubs? Very simply, it's because dogs shed, and it's important for our members to look elegant and well-maintained.

Recruiting recently around the city, I came across a frightening experience. A large man in a green suit casually tossed a match into the gas tank of a parked car. The car exploded into flames, lighting up the man's face to reveal a wide grin. It occurred to me that fire is an intriguing front of nature-battle that might be immune to Goose Club preparation. I can see the beginning of an argument somewhere here:

1. We are, as humans, in pursuit of the ideal dog.

2. Quite simply, fire is an ideal dog.

Obviously, it's only the beginning. If you are, or might be, engaging in enthusiastic fire battle, please contact me for professional advice.

Certainly this composition would bring the lovely Carolina to my door. I leaned back, satisfied.

My room was spacious, with high ceilings and double glass doors leading to a little sunroom where I could eat a peaceful breakfast, though I rarely found occasion to. It had big windows and, outside, a hallway so pleasant that I often left my door ajar. But my room would always cause me dissatisfaction. There were only two corners in which to put my bed; the others either had radiators or were too near to doors. There was only one place to put my desk, because it had to be by windows and near enough to electrical outlets, but this one location was too close to one of the potential bed corners. Therefore, I was left with no choice when it came to the arrangement of my important pieces of furniture and could not put a bookshelf near my bed because of a window, nor could I install a couch because of where my bathroom was. It would be wrong to say that my room caused me real despair, but it would also be wrong to give a description of my room without complaining about it.

I chewed on a scrap of toast and wondered idly about what had become of Reath. Had he recovered the disreputable prints? Because Grel would probably have the news, I decided to go to his place as soon as I dropped off my column.

I dreaded speaking to Mavil's father without positive progress, given that he was an impatient sort of person not noticeably tuned to comedy. He was short and wide with clothes that fit him so tightly that it was hard to comfortably look at him. His favorite color was blue; each article he wore carried some of that color, but not in any matching shades. Luckily, he was rich enough to appear as he did.

The man had pulled me aside a few days ago, as I slipped out from Mavil's nursery to look at the sky while she worked a few problems.

"Charfo, update," he brusquely requested.

"We're doing algebra. Mavil's quite good at it."

"How abstract?"

"I'm sorry," I replied, confused. "I introduce word problems from time to time, so it's not too abstract."

"I want her to learn the abstract algebra."

"Oh, I see what you mean. Well, the plan is to teach elementary algebra first, then trigonometry and calculus before abstract algebra."

"She's only on elementary algebra?"

"That's advanced for her age," I explained.

"When given a problem involving a lot of money and unknown amounts of coins, does my daughter get confused?"

"Mavil's very adept at such problems."

"But do her eyes wander while she thinks?"

"Her eyes are very focused."

"Does my daughter often ask a lot of questions in order to disrupt your lectures?"

Mavil did ask a lot of questions unrelated to the subject of the day, but I didn't mind. Even if the questioning was a tactic to prevent me from speaking about exponents and logarithms, she genuinely seemed interested in the answers I gave. A teacher teaches best by answering questions, and, honestly, I didn't mind getting distracted from exponents and logarithms.

"Mavil behaves very well," I replied diplomatically.

"When eating her sandwich at lunchtime, does my daughter read from cheap novels?"

"She reads the dialogues of very good philosophers."

"When questioned about virtue, does my daughter blush?"

"Your daughter replies with confidence and provides references."

"Does my daughter write notes in perfumed envelopes and ask her maid to deliver them to the house down the road?"

"To my knowledge, besides letters to her brother in the army, she writes only treatises," I lied.

"Charfo, I'm a busy man."

He didn't continue, which left me in an uncomfortable position. I thought that it was very possible he was angry with me or had seen through my lies. I considered saying, "I understand, I'll double my efforts," but I worried he'd think me too servile. I wrung my hands behind my back and swallowed repeatedly. I could hear the sound of Mavil's pen scratching on paper in the other room.

I wondered how many interesting clouds I'd already missed because of this conversation. It was civil twilight, which is the best time to look outside. Once at such a time, I'd seen a wonderful blanket of nacreous clouds above the quiet shadow of the city. I'd taught very distractedly afterward. My fidgeting hands found my cloud diary in my back pocket, and I ran my fingers nervously over its worn spine until Mavil's father broke the silence.

"I'm glad you understand. Have them for me next week."

I did not understand, but nodded slowly.

"If you're absent, where should I leave them?" I ventured.

"Slide them into my locked drawer. That's the top one in my desk. You're a wise man, Charfo."

He began to walk away; I didn't know how to get any more information without disappointing the man with respect to my character. In my anxiety, I thought of causing some commotion with the nearby vases but didn't have the courage. Mavil's father disappeared up the stairs.

I was seriously dejected and only barely made it through the rest of my lesson with Mavil. While she recited poetry from a great master, I stared down at the floor without blinking or thinking clearly about anything. Mavil asked me to tell her the meaning of a few words from her reading, but in my state I wasn't able to remember the definitions. At the time, I thought it best to tell her they weren't English. I can only hope that when she comes across the meanings later she'll think it a good joke.

Finally, by the time I'd packed up my books and stepped out into the cool air, my composure was slightly restored. I took a seat on a bench in the family's garden and thought my way to two conclusions: one, I should always take the other door out of Mavil's nursery, for that route had a much smaller chance of me running into anyone; and two, I needed to sneak into Mavil's father's study and to break into his locked drawer in order to find out what sort of thing he wanted me to get for him. Needless to say, when I looked in the drawer, I found a very tidy pile of pornographic photographs. I also found a small gun, a bottle of milk, two dead crickets, and a box of nail clippings with blue polish on them. The key to the drawer, oddly enough, had been sitting in the lock.

*

Leaning dangerously far back in my chair, the last shred of toast dangling from my teeth, I was roused by a knock at my door. Sarah Beeley came in. She wore a loose red scarf with gold trim, and her dark hair was wildly styled to be up and down at the same time. I admired her while she unabashedly examined my room. Sarah worked for a company that developed innovative birdseeds, and her job was to collect facts. She spent most of her time interviewing elderly couples and writing down their beliefs about grain ratios and the effects of weather conditions on avian appetites. I wanted to kiss her; she had the most wonderful nose in profile.

"I thought you never drank milk."

She was pointing at the bottle on my desk, the one Mrs. Fiss had given me the night before.

"It was a gift. I don't think it's milk. I think it's slum swill or whatever that stuff they make in prisons is called."

"Slop?"

"I think that's what prisoners call their food."

"Have you tasted it?"

"I was saving it for something special," I decided that instant. "We can taste it when I solve one of the mysteries I'm working on."

"You've mysteries?"

"Sarah, I have literally fifty-six conversations' worth of things to tell you."

"I've got a lot to tell you, too," she replied.

In the following silence, I wondered what to tell Sarah. I wanted to tell her everything, but I didn't know where to begin.

"You haven't tried on your costume."

The package lay at the foot of my bed, where I'd evidently dropped it the night before. I righted my chair and went to unpack it.

"There's a lot of news about you," she said behind me. "But I haven't paid it much attention. I've been out screaming at the world."

The wizard costume consisted of a deep blue robe with sparkling patterns somehow printed onto it and an ingeniously collapsible conical hat. It could be flattened, but, left alone, it would spring to its full two-foot height. I immediately put the hat on. A number of accessories were also included: a flimsy wand with a tassel—or was it a wrist strap?—a faux-jeweled necklace, an aged spellbook which seemed to be a renovated foreign dictionary, and astrological plastic trinkets attached to a leather belt.

"I had to meet an old woman and her husband at a mall," Sarah said. "They spend all their time there, apparently, and the woman was supposed to know just the right combination of corn and banana to attract talkative mockingbirds. Pin, from here on out, I'm going to exaggerate what happened and probably also flat out lie, in order to convey my feelings."

"Naturally," I offhanded.

The robe fit well, and I looked an admirable and competent wizard in the mirror. Still, I didn't like the idea of the costume, and I felt compelled to disrupt Sarah's plans. I contemplated whether or not I could manage to wear the wizard hat with a deer hunter costume; I really liked the hat.

"I didn't get very far in my questioning before I heard a commotion on the floor above," Sarah continued. "It's a mall, so there are all sorts of indoor courtyard features with balconies. The mall also has a large window on one wall which I'll get to later. There were many voices above me, mostly angry. I excused myself from the woman and her husband and took an escalator up a floor."

Sarah stood in the middle of the room, using her hands to stage the story she told. I put the wizard costume away and went to sit on my desk in order to listen. I then noticed a package of photographs behind the milk bottle. A rectangular piece of paper was tucked under the rubber band holding them together. A little typewritten note was printed on it:

Pictures of Bruth Cormill

June 18

I met Bruth Cormill on a trip back in November. He sat next to me in a terribly decorated cafe. We started talking after he asked for the ketchup, and we ended up discussing municipal water systems. Bruth's a fun guy. We're good friends now.

The photographs showed a squat little man with curly blond hair in an auto mechanic's uniform. In an upraised hand, he held a very large wrench. The portraits had all been taken at the same time in what appeared to be a children's corn maze. This new Cormill was much less pleasing than the one from last night, and it wasn't simply the lack of an ostentatious suitcase: Bruth smiled with an extravagance only found in the expressions of clueless villains. I decided to think about him later.

"It was a brawl," Sarah went on. "Limbs were striking in every direction. The mass of shouting people looked like that tangle you find on the beach, writhing in the surf. I was pushed from behind by an energetic arm and soon found myself in the middle of the fray and then suddenly on the ground with stomping feet in every direction.

"It's difficult to describe the time that passed from that point to the point when it all stopped, when we were all strewn about the floor, whining and moaning at no one in particular. I remember ripping clothes and digging my nails into flesh. I remember making it back to my feet and hurling someone over the guardrail—they landed a floor below, near the pretzel cart. Many people were hurled off into the void like that, and they came back up to hurl other people off. In the end, I found myself missing a sock, in a man's leather jacket, stuffed upside down in a trash can.

"A hand with a shard of glass in it was shaking me awake. I felt around to confirm that all my parts were attached and discovered that a child was in the trash can with me, whimpering and holding wads of bills in her clenched fists. The hand directed me back to the focal point of the recent battle where the participants were politely gathering together again, exhausted, around a pile of upturned benches.

"A woman in a business suit and broken heels clambered up the wreckage and motioned for quiet, though the only real sounds were from people in too much pain to be paying any attention in the first place. 'We've deliberated and decided on the following: every brawler will be given a five-minute period in which to share with the rest of us the reasons for their participation.' Her hair was a blood-matted mess, and she was missing a tooth. As she spoke, she would frequently pause to feel the space with her tongue. 'What gives you the authority?' someone called before lapsing into a bout of coughing from the effort. 'The Brawl Initiation Committee brought me in as a consultant, back when the Committee's president was battered over the head with a mannequin.' There was whispering, and a man lying under a fake fern shouted, 'It really hurt!' At his side, a woman in a tattered skirt and half a pair of spectacles transcribed the man's words while mopping his brow with a little stuffed tiger. 'We'll go in alphabetical order to help Ms. Dinjer's records,' the consultant nodded in the woman's direction. Ms. Dinjer gave a thumbs up and then quickly returned to her shorthand.

"Pin?"

"Yes?"

I'd been listening closely but staring into the milk bottle at the same time. The liquid inside looked like a watery oil spill. Very quickly I wondered why it was that I didn't feel more overwhelmed by recent events. Was my character developing, or was I simply under more anxiety than I'd ever experienced?

"I'm just going to summarize the monologues if that's okay. Most of them are made up anyway."

I nodded and saluted.

Sarah came over and sat beside me on the desk before continuing. The floor of my room was dappled by sunlight passing through the tall elms outside; it was thin late-afternoon sunlight.

"I curled up in a big pile of soft popcorn from an overturned cart and listened to the explanations. Greble Attisop: 'Last month, my mother died and left me a whole lot of money, so I bought a car. Now that people don't fall asleep on my shoulder to and from work, I need to go out of my way to touch other humans.' Shing Breft: 'As we sing, so must we dance. Also I was, and still am, considerably drunk from last night.' Wessel Cooling: 'I reject the Committee and its brawl regulations. I reject these motive monologues. I was the one who first struck the president over the head with the mannequin. The others followed my example.' Ben Dextriss: 'I saw a child dropping gum wrappers on the floor in full view of her smoothie-drinking mother whose only reaction was to follow suit and drop her straw wrapper on the floor.' Ress Eschepleque: 'It causes me sincere pain to find out that we still aren't teaching children the scientific names of animals.' Chin Fricklong: 'Someone severed my nylon cord so I've lost my fellows. Are any of you my fellows?' Qwith Goode: 'I was trained to fight skillfully back in my homeland. I seek out conflict in order to stay in good form. Notice, I have very few bruises and lacerations.' Nivesh Hulm: 'Yesterday, I finally realized that I don't like governments. This is my first time out in public with my new anarchist ideals. I was the second person to hit the Committee's president over the head.' Zap Ieger: 'Love, you see, made me very upset.' Ethan Jithe: 'I'm one of your fellows, Chin! Tie up to me. I'm also connected to that unconscious man over there.' Tucine Kasley: 'A man ahead of me in the popcorn line used the phrase *social lubricant*, so naturally I punched him in the gut.' Extring Lum: 'I'm a nasty man. When all this commotion started going on around me, I took the opportunity to press my private parts against the nearest lady.' A'Im Mendo: 'My reading comprehension has been decaying; I can no longer manage the complicated, foreign novels I used to read with my breakfast. I'm almost to the stage where I can't handle anything without cute illustrations. My friends quote things I don't understand.' Rep Nundudder: 'Fighting used to be part of my curriculum at school, but it got removed by the boring people before I could register for the class.' Todd Oventimer: 'I collect socks. These socks in my pockets I stole from your feet when you were distracted or burnt out. In this jar, I have a bunch of coins which I'm going to distribute as compensation.' Kathling Positive: 'I was the third person to strike the president in the head with the mannequin. I did it because I saw Nivesh do it, and I decided I liked the aesthetic. Maybe I'll do it to a real president some day. I think that would make me content.' Hast Qinti: 'Instead of talking about my motives, I'm going to respond to Mr. Dextriss. Sir, I'm the littering child's father and the littering woman's husband. I taught my child that it's morally correct to litter. Was this a big mistake?' Meik Roofthispelt: 'Six years ago at a beach house, I saw a bright object in the sky and heard a strange siren. I woke up in the morning with this radioactive tattoo. I firmly believe that I experienced aliens. I also believe in interspecies telepathic communication.' Trev Subtraa: 'What country do I live in? When did that tree behind my garage fall over? Or, was it cut down by a revolutionary element? Where did I put my daughter? Will my messed-up toenail ever grow normally again?' Eth Tryx: 'I'll expound on my opinion of colors. It's very easy for me to say I like a color, but difficult for me to say I dislike one. This might lead to an interesting idea, but instead of going in that direction I'm going to list all of the colors in the order in which I like them. My favorite is red, then orange, then white, then yellow, then gray, then green, then black, then brown, then purple, then blue.' Owney Umtrilass: 'Honestly, I didn't realize I was in a brawl. I thought it was a very contact-oriented dance party. In college, I learned to enjoy dancing, but now that I'm old it's hard for me to find places where I'll be welcomed into the fun. In a few years, I probably won't be able to walk—especially now that my leg is very broken—and I don't want to go to wheelchair dances because they never play the music I like.' Carol Vax: 'I heard a couple on a bench discussing television very loudly, but they weren't saying anything interesting. Other people passing by joined in, because the couple seemed so friendly, but still no one said anything interesting. I tried to talk to one of them about taxonomy, but she turned away.' Den Wischnutcario: 'Let me confess something: I don't like the taste of our drink. I usually keep it in a bag so that I can easily puncture holes in it and get away with saying that it leaked out. I tried quitting the league but I couldn't undo all of the knots.' O Xetipode: 'I ordered a sandwich without mayonnaise but the guy put mayonnaise in it. I brought it back, and he made another one for me but put mayonnaise in that one, too. I asked him if he was all right, and he said that he wasn't.' Mati Yuck: 'I was the fourth person to strike the president with the mannequin. I'm not supposed to be here, so I wanted to fit in. I went to the wrong address and am now too embarrassed to go to the right one. I just want a girlfriend.' Aeurollae Zeitho: 'It's ridiculously annoying that I have to pay for things I want. I never want anything extreme. I got yelled at earlier for sitting on the floor. Why can't we sit on the floor in the mall? In some countries, the emperor sits on the floor. Are those countries more advanced, or am I not of emperor stock? Given the chance, I would rephrase that question.'"

"Didn't you explain yourself to them?" I asked.

"Of course, we all had to say something. For my turn, I pointed through the wide window in the wall and exclaimed about how big the building across the road was. It was an enormous building. I've never seen anything bigger. Why was it there? I said that I should never have to see a building so big in the course of my life. I even threw a chair at the window for emphasis, though nothing broke."

"Sarah?"

"Pin?"

"Tomorrow, at the party, can we stand next to each other?"

"Of course."

She ruffled my hair, took a book from my nightstand, and made a hasty exit.

*

My column hand-off went smoothly, and I soon found myself in front of Grel's apartment building, sweating in the humid air. The sky was already darkening, but no breeze accompanied it. It felt more like the deliberate arrival of a patient superstorm than the stifling evening it was, though the domestic railing from the windows above contradicted the idea; no one quarrels in the shadow of a natural disaster. A husband seemed to have set fire to all of his wife's undergarments, though the reason was still unclear.

"I'll go get Grel for you," a dirty boy in a homemade cape offered.

"I'd be much obliged," I answered, giving the child a coin.

He didn't move. "Your name's Pinson Charfo, right?"

"Yes, call me Pin. A lot of people call me Charfo, but I don't like it at all."

"Last night, a man with a funny suitcase came by looking for you."

The description sounded like Mr. Cormill—Sefting Cormill, not Bruth Cormill, who only had a big wrench. Last night, while I'd been in Mr. Selmare's basement, Mr. Cormill had gone to my apartment. Maybe he'd come looking for me here after that. Maybe Mrs. Fiss had suggested the idea. Tangentially, I wondered if Drea were real, because it seemed like the strange slum people from Grel's story were real. Maybe she was hiding up there in one of the windows. Back on track, I wondered if I'd somehow switched the photographs in my sleep. That seemed unlikely, though, considering I probably did less in my sleep than I hoped. Maybe the photographs were the kind they used in birthday cards that changed over time. But how had they managed to get untangled from my bedclothes? I didn't like the idea, but someone must have come into my room last night, and it probably wasn't their first time.

"Can you just go get Grel?"

"Sure thing, boss. But, can I have your watch instead of this coin?"

"No, you can't have my watch. What are you supposed to be anyway?" I asked, pointing at his cape.

"I'm Monopo."

Monopo, from the picture in the photograph cellar! But this kid didn't look like the Monopo I remembered. I felt around desperately in my pockets even though I was certain I'd left the picture behind, in the lake. My hands really wanted to help, but it was a mind matter, a memory matter; seeing them expend so much effort for no possible reward was a little melancholic.

"I thought Monopo had a grisly ear."

"No, that's Clothus. Monopo has a cape."

"What's yours made from, a canvas sack?"

"A nyloner from the movement gave it to me. I traded him for it. I gave him a cork to plug his bottle of booze. Monopo's real cape is velvet. People call it his *black velvet cape*, but it's really a regal dark purple. It came from a king, a real king."

"And Clothus, what really happened to his ear?"

"Only Monopo knows. Clothus doesn't even, which is

a little weird to me. I've never hurt myself and not known about it. Have you ever tasted your own blood?"

"Yes. It's not particularly noteworthy."

"Orphel, at the sandpits, says that Clothus hurt his ear by experimenting with villainy. Is it possible for villainy to do that to your ear? I want to be a villain, but I don't want to hurt myself being one."

"Villainy can do an awful lot, but it's usually not so bad for your ears. What's your real name?"

"Squail, boss."

"Squail, this Orphel doesn't know what he's talking about."

The urchin stood at attention. Urchins were fascinated by soldiers; they always created regiments and chaos. I gave Squail another coin—he'd need something to lose in a bet—and motioned for him to go inside.

"Pin, if you find any purple velvet in your adventures . . ." he trailed off as he disappeared into the wretched residence.

Grel was dapper and smelled flowery. He arranged his scarf nervously and explained that he was just on his way out. He wouldn't tell me where. I asked if Drea was involved, and he replied, "Of course." I complained that I wanted to take him to dinner, but my protests didn't seem to make an impression.

"Grel, any news of Reath, then?"

"Absolutely nothing. I've been out looking for him twice today and bribed armies of these street children to fact-find. Mr. Selmare's shop is locked up tight. There's more to talk about, but I've got to go."

"What about?"

"The stolen manifesto. Bernsy's gone crazy. He's started dressing in all black and throwing pens at people who don't listen to him. And I'm close to joining him, seeing as your followers keep wrecking my room."

"My followers?" I repeated. "I honestly know nothing about this thing or its followers. People think I've written it, but I've never even read it."

"That's comforting but strange. We'll discuss this tomorrow. I'm going to be late."

"I'll walk with you."

"I'm taking a car," he said as he hailed a cab.

"I'll come by before the party tomorrow, then. We need to make sense of that boat ride, too," I replied before he sped away.

For a time I stood, reveling in my confusion, Squail at

attention by my side. There was a lot to think about, but I chose to drift above it all, feeling the delicate prickle of the mysteries' extremities. I visualized the conglomerate of questions as a green sea urchin, but an unnatural sort of green you only find in a child's coloring box. I considered that I might be scuba diving with green-tinted goggles. You know, I told myself, that tinted glasses greatly affect your mood, and mood, they say, is absolutely vital to maintain while isolated at the bottom of the sea. But the question of why I was scuba diving in the metaphor was in itself quite a mystery, and if that question were also part of the urchin, what did that mean for my metaphor? How did I expect to make sense of anything if I got stuck in mindspaces of this sort? Was that question also part of the urchin? Was *that* question also part of the urchin? Was *that* question also part of the urchin?

Finally, I stirred awake and asked the way to Mr. Evesong's costume shop. Squail directed me to it for another coin.

*

In my experience—around the city mostly, since foreign places are too distracting to remember very well—I'd come to see costume shops as simply more exciting clothing stores, which was not a positive thing because, typically, clothing stores were ruined by the presence of attentive salespeople and bad selections. Mr. Evesong's shop was called *Costumes* and was nestled into a quiet part of the city without restaurants and abrasive strangers. The door jingled as I entered. Mr. Evesong presented himself before I could escape deeper into the store.

"I'm looking for a deer hunter's costume," I told him reluctantly.

"There are deer hunting costumes over here," he replied, helpfully motioning past something ugly and colorful, like an exploded poisonous frog.

I went over to look where Mr. Evesong had indicated and was disappointed to find that he'd followed me. He waited patiently for my opinion.

"This is too much camo, really," I said. "Do deer hunters need all this camo?"

"When you're deer hunting, you want to be able to blend into the trees so that the deer you're hunting won't see you very well."

"Do deer see very well?" I asked.

"Generally, I suppose, they must."

"I read a book about safaris once, and the author never mentioned camo, only khaki and mosquito boots."

"Then what you want is a kudu hunter's costume. Those are over here."

"Wait," I stopped the enthusiastic man. "I want to be a deer hunter. I just thought my safari comment was interesting."

"I think it was confusing. You wouldn't hunt deer on safari."

"A deer hunter would."

Mr. Evesong didn't respond and scratched behind an ear; he appeared to have lost the direction of our conversation.

"The trouble is," I clarified, "that these clothes all seem like the sort of stuff the general population would wear to go deer hunting, while I'm looking more for the costume of a deer hunter: a man who very often hunts deer and is not a member of the general population, because the general population only hunts deer on occasion or never even at all."

The man brightened after internalizing this idea. "A deer stalker's what you want."

"I worry that everyone would think I'm a detective."

He was confused again, I could see, and went on in ignorance of my joke. It was clear that Mr. Selmare was the clever one in their partnership.

"A deer stalker is the real professional. My grandfather used to correct me when I used the word 'hunt' because that was supposed to be the word for what you did with hounds from the back of a horse. Now it doesn't matter so much because everything's all mixed together, like those children whose fathers went off to war and came back with native women."

I coughed.

"What you want is a rifle. I can get you a toy one that shoots little pellets. I'll glue a telescope on the top. I've plenty from my astronomer sets. Then, you'll need buckskins and a brimmed hat."

"Buckskins with fringe?" I asked.

"I can do that, but it'll be an additional charge. Real deer stalkers have fringe, that's true."

"This is great. When can I pick it up?"

"Since it's a custom design, I'll need to assemble it. Can you come back in a week?"

"I've only a day."

Mr. Evesong was displeased. "I take my work very seriously."

"I'm sorry it's such short notice. I've been really busy."

"I have been too. You'd be astonished to know the number of people coming in here looking for wizard costumes for tomorrow night."

"There's a costume party at an important guy's house, that's why. He's sort of a jerk, though."

"I suspected as much," he said to himself, though I wasn't sure to which sentence he was referring.

"So, will you be able to make the costume for me in time?"

"Yes, I can," he said unhappily.

We settled the cost to something shockingly high, but I used Ralfo's check to make it affordable. While Mr. Evesong was writing out the receipt and doing other necessary bureaucracy, I explored the shop. In the back corner behind a rack of yoga suits and leotards, I found a staircase leading downstairs to a big, black cellar that reminded me of Mr. Selmare's. It echoed eerily, and I felt the chill of my recent swim washing over my shoulders. I hurried back upstairs into the warm light.

"I'll be by tomorrow afternoon," I said to Mr. Evesong.

He muttered back and continued to write notes on the list of items we'd deemed necessary for my costume. On the way out, I hesitated in the doorway, wishing to stay a moment longer in the comforting glow of Mr. Evesong's overhead lights; the street looked tauntingly like the interior of the basement. Once outside, though, the notion dissipated instantly in the warm night air.

I didn't want to go home, so I wandered around with the idea of eventually ending up in a cafe. The streets I found were unfamiliar and irregular and were even cobbled at times. The houses to either side leaned down toward me as if bowing, but I didn't get the sense that they were doing it out of any sincere respect; rather, perhaps, because they were spineless. From their windows, I heard a number of late evening activities: hushed discussions about finances that rose unexpectedly to volumes which made the children upstairs stir in their sleep; slurred philosophy from downstairs common rooms full of dense smoke and dizzying smells; emphatic advice from elders directed at the silhouettes of delicately nodding heads. It all made me feel increasingly lonely, and by the time the light of a midnight diner struck me, as a spotlight, in the center of the empty street, I realized I was shuffling, squinting, and rapidly running my hands through my hair. I went inside and ordered coffee and a plate of fries.

I was the only customer in the diner, but the chrome lining of the interior shone so cleanly that I saw myself in every corner; I was sitting on the stool at the counter, at the booth by the cigarette dispenser, on the sign by the bathroom, and in my pot of cream. I didn't want the cream, and I put a napkin in front of it so I wouldn't see myself in it. The fries were good and crispy.

"You have the eyes of someone," the waitress said to me when she came to refill my coffee.

Without invitation, she sat down across from me. She was a baggy woman in a dark brown apron, and when she sat, she let out a long sigh. I wasn't sure if the sigh was from exhaustion or love sickness or frustration—the difference in sound has always been too subtle for me—but I found it annoying; why was she expressing her emotions like that?

"Whose eyes do I have?"

"That's what I'm remembering. It's on the tip of my brain."

The waitress held up a finger and stared intently at

me, but I soon realized she wasn't looking at me as much as into her own mind, so I took the opportunity to drink my coffee and eat a few fries.

"My husband, that's who. He was a decent guy, really. At first I thought your eyes were like my alderman's, the ones he had back when I was seeing him, though. We had a wonderful time back then. We would go to the boardwalk every night, and he'd give me all of the prizes he won. Now his eyes are different, and he says seeing me is against his religion. But having a religion is against my religion, so there's that issue. I dreamt about him last night, really!" She blushed. "I won't share it. It's one of those dirty dreams that make you glad you're sleeping alone and no one's there to watch you."

"So, the alderman wasn't your husband?"

"No, no. My husband's been off and on. He goes through phases, and I go through phases, and only one in a hundred of them involves affection. I mean serious, down-on-the-ground affection."

"That's too bad. Was it different in the beginning?"

"I can't remember, but it must have been. I married him, after all."

The waitress had brought this conversation to me

while I'd just wanted to eat my fries, but it felt like she was expecting me to keep it going. I smiled pleasantly, but she wouldn't get up and leave.

"This coffee is terrible," I said.

She looked horrified and made a deep sucking sound with her face before taking the cup from me and frowning down into it.

"It looks all right, but maybe something's not right."

"It tastes like plastic."

"I know just what you mean. I chew on pens when I'm in the state, you know. It's not healthy because everyone uses my pens to sign their bills."

"Is this coffee supposed to taste like plastic?" I asked.

"I think so. It's very cheap."

"Do you have more expensive coffee?"

"No, no one would buy it."

"I would."

"Would you?" she asked.

"Well, when I get an impulsive urge, like tonight."

"We can't run a business on that!" the waitress argued. "And, anyway, you're the only one who's said anything about it in months. A guy came in here last week and drank seven cups in thirty minutes."

"What did he look like?"

"I don't know, thin." The waitress stood up. "What does it matter?"

I shrugged.

"You've a face, though, wow," she exclaimed.

I tried to find something to read in order to look busy, but the newspapers were far away, and I didn't have a book in my pocket.

"Where are you from?" the waitress asked.

"Here. I live over the river."

"No, I mean originally. Where were you born?"

"Here. Over the river. I've moved about six blocks, although in between I went away to school."

"Where'd you get that accent from, then?"

"I don't have an accent."

"It's a strange way to talk. You're sure it's not an accent?"

"I'm sure. No one ever mentions it," I replied.

"Then it's a speech impediment."

"I don't know what you're talking about."

The waitress was very insistent.

"You keep putting your vowels in the wrong places. You put them all over while they're only supposed to be in certain places," she explained.

"What?"

"It's like there's a howling sound behind your voice sometimes. But I've checked, and it's coming from your mouth. It's a part of your voice."

I was confused. It occurred to me that this was maybe her odd way of flirting, but it certainly wasn't working. Or maybe the problem with my voice was with her ears, instead. In the newspaper, I'd recently read about a man who one day discovered he was blind in one eye. When they investigated it, they found that it wasn't anything new; he'd apparently been blind in the eye for years and just never noticed.

"Say something," the waitress commanded. "Let me hear it again."

"I don't know what to say. There really isn't a problem with my voice."

The waitress cooed, "Wow, what a voice! I want to record it. Let me get my radio."

She hurried away into the kitchen. I took the opportunity to throw some bills on the table and run for the door. I hadn't finished my fries, but I wasn't going to be able to finish them anyway—there'd been an awful lot on the plate. Just as I reached out for the door handle, the door opened inwards and I was forced into a plant to avoid colliding with a new customer. For a moment, everything was green, and I thrashed around in order to organize my person. Even before I was back on my feet, though, a distinctive fungal smell entered my nose, and I knew at once who'd come in.

"Charfo!" cried Reath in surprise.

He'd undergone some sort of strange transformation since I'd seen him last in the photograph shop. He was groomed and well-dressed and carried a stuffed file folder under his arm like a businessman. His nose even seemed to have inflated a little, such that it took on a more noble outline. But the smell persisted, and I noticed that his socks were mismatched and loose.

"I really was . . . I really did intend to come by and see you first thing," Reath stammered. "But I've been so busy, so caught up in it. I can see you understand. Good! I was so worried you'd beat the living . . . Well, I can see that you forgive me and that you'd always forgive me. I should never have thought otherwise. I really haven't thought otherwise. It's just the activity of it all, you see. I lost my principles. I forgot them in the chaos. I'm so glad you understand."

I didn't understand, but I knew right away from this sort of speech that he wasn't up to anything good. The transformation was a farce.

"I can't tell you how glad I am to see you here," Reath continued, frantically looking around at the interior of the diner. "I was going to visit you after my coffee, honestly. It's a wonderful coincidence! It brings to mind the quote from Clipshaw: 'Coincidence reconciles cognitive conflict.'"

"That's not Clipshaw. Clipshaw was the astronaut who burned up on reentry. Maybe you're thinking of Misteng's quote, though if so, you butchered it."

"You're right; it was Melissa! You have a skill, Charfo, a big bunch of bananas."

"Misteng, not Melissa. Who's Melissa?"

"Melissa, the . . ."

Reath was interrupted by an explosion of verbal abuse from somewhere behind me. I jumped back and took refuge in my booth and watched as the waitress stormed from behind the counter, spewing insults and grievances, lashing out violently at Reath. At first, Reath groveled disgustingly at the woman's feet—even going so far as to suck her toes—and patiently bore the blows, but eventually it dawned on him that the woman saw straight through his antics, and he was soon jumping around, shouting vitriol, and throwing dishes at the walls. A row of cooks filed out from the kitchen and watched with amusement from the safety of the counter.

I gathered, while cowering in my corner to avoid ceramics, that Reath was the husband the waitress had recently told me about, and the waitress was the wife who'd recently left Reath. I learned that the waitress's name was Chevsa and that they'd had three children together, which came as a shock to me, because that made Grel an uncle. The two had met in a gambling hall; Chevsa was there disposing of some illegal income, and Reath occupied her elbow, supplying tips for tips. When the money ran out, they discovered that they were married. It wasn't clear to me how this had happened because they both accused the other of confidence tricking, but my guess was that they'd each attempted some scam. It was also quite possible their marriage had been caused by a clerical error, or maybe they'd accidentally signed the wrong paper while taking out a loan, for these two demonstrated no lifestyle strengths. Since their marriage, Reath and Chevsa had organized a number of schemes and heists but had subsequently failed to enact them successfully. Reath was back to share his latest one. Between blows and detractions, he explained how he'd deftly managed to gain the trust of the city's top distributor of disreputable prints and how he was in a unique position to "harvest the stuff."

Chevsa was unimpressed. "You're extremely fat."

"You're a toad, but that doesn't ruin my plan."

"But your fat will ruin it. You'll lose the best pictures in your fat crevices."

Reath dashed a plate at his feet and stomped over to a table. He began to unpack his file folder, laying packets of photographs out on the table with trembling hands. Chevsa threw a pitcher of water at him, but it missed and ruined a napkin dispenser. I didn't care to wait around to see the resolution of this quarrel.

"Reath, if you don't mind, I'll just take my forty percent and get out of here."

Reath looked up from his display with a shell-shocked expression, huffing from the yelling and throwing.

"We arranged that I'd get forty percent of the prints we stole," I clarified. "To make things easy, though, you can just give me one of those stacks."

"Charfo, Charfo, of course!"

I could tell Reath wanted to get rid of me. He tossed me a packet of prints and then promptly dove for cover behind the hostess stand. I thumbed my way through the photographs to make sure he hadn't duped me. It was a good thing I did.

"Reath, the last two of these photos are really not disreputable at all. This woman is fully clothed, and this photo's so dark I can only see a leg."

"But that's the idea. I cut the goods! I replace two in every twelve with tame stuff, and I end up with two in every twelve as profit. It's brilliant if you—"

I lost his voice behind Chevsa's war cry as she charged Reath's barricade with a stanchion. I figured ten saucy prints would be enough and escaped through the door before things got worse.

*

I don't read bad books, but sometimes I'll start one and then throw it away. I go to plays, but when they inevitably turn bad, I leave the theater and get a drink. I go to art museums, but I don't look at anything—usually I go to meet someone in the dining area. I was walking home that night, coming up with these sorts of sentences, and it dawned on me that I felt fantastic; I shouted, incoherently. It was because I had the prints in my pocket, I decided, though I knew that wasn't quite the right reason. A policeman approached me from across the street, and because I didn't want to bother explaining my manic outcry, I dodged into an alley and through the rear of a movie theater. The film was bad, but I didn't stay to critique it fairly.

Mrs. Fiss was on the stoop when I got home.

"Good evening," I greeted.

"The Pin returns!" she cried and raised an empty hand in a toast.

I imitated the gesture, and we touched knuckles as she made a poor impression of glasses clinking.

"You've gone dry?"

"The shipment was attacked by pirates," which was Mrs. Fiss's way of saying that her peglegged friends had come by and helped her to finish her daily ration. "But it doesn't matter now. I'm content. Those junkyard people were back for your signature. I told them you were out and they got very insistent. Very insistent. I called Mr. Katto down and we chased them off. They left you this milk bottle of their sauce. That makes two, unless you finished the first."

"I haven't. But I'm going to drink it as soon as I get up there," I said, pointing to my window.

Mrs. Fiss chuckled. "And Sarah wanted me to ask if you solved any of your cases."

"I did," I said, flashing the packet of disreputable prints. "That's why I'm celebrating. Is she up there?"

"Yep. I don't think she sleeps, you know."

"That's very plausible."

I contemplated how plausible that actually was and ended up being very unconvinced; I'd seen her sleeping. She could have been faking it, but that would have been a hard thing to do given the length of time. In any case, everyone could be faking everything, but I didn't think it was necessary to consider that particular scenario in these circumstances.

"Thanks, I'm off. Last words?" I said.

"Pinson, dear, you're charming. Go slow at the milk bottle. It's strong stuff. Take quinine if you start to see spots. I'm serious, put a bottle of quinine in your breast pocket. And Pinson, you don't have to marry the girl, but at least run away to some faraway place with her."

Upstairs, I found Sarah reading. I invited her to my room. We sat on the bed, and while she doodled in the margin of her book—she always read with a pen in hand—I explained the mission Mavil's father had given me and how, with the help of Grel and Reath, I'd resolved it. Naturally, Sarah was most interested in the underground lake and the photograph landscape.

"Did all of the water come from the leaky fountain?"

"I'm not sure. It's very extensive down there."

"But if it is all from the fountain, then won't the rest of the photograph world eventually flood?"

"That's not necessarily true," I said. "There could be some outlet up on the wall, like the holes they have in sink basins."

Sarah laid back, letting the book fall gracefully from her hands, and stared up at my ceiling as she tied small knots in her hair. The cracks and irregularities up on the ceiling formed a multitude of little characters and landscapes, which I'd identified in that lost time before falling asleep. I wondered how many of my discoveries Sarah noticed, and how many of them Sarah interpreted as something completely different.

"Pin, take me down there," she dreamily commanded.

I was tired, but I hadn't been awake long enough to justify sleep. I supposed it was a good idea to bring Sarah down into that subterranean mystery.

"Sure, let's do it. But let's celebrate my accomplishment first." I pointed at my two bottles of slum slosh. "Do you have any quinine?"

"How do you know Mavil's dad wanted those prints? Maybe he wanted something else. Maybe he wanted you to get him more nail clippings or dead crickets. Maybe your mission isn't over."

Sarah had tied a strong loop of hair around her left index finger, and as she sat up, her finger remained suspended next to her head. I couldn't help myself from smiling at her. She laughed back at me in a beautiful way.

"I believe it's over, and he isn't here to contradict me. That's how truth works."

"And why do we need quinine?"

"In case things go bad with the drink. Mrs. Fiss suggested it. She knows her stuff."

While Sarah ransacked her bathroom for the quinine bottle she knew was in there somewhere, I opened one of the milk bottles and inhaled deeply. The smell exploded in my nostrils—alcohol, dust, and chlorine—and I discovered myself, some short time later, in a coughing fit at the foot of my bed. By then, Sarah was back and investigating the other milk bottle in a more prudent fashion.

"This smells incredibly unhealthy," she reported.

We took small sips, covering our noses at first, and found that it tasted even worse than we'd expected, but that it felt very good in our stomachs and in our heads. Soon we were staggering out past Mrs. Fiss and down to Tisholong Bridge, bottles under our arms.

According to my memory of the excursion, we walked beneath a bright blue sky spotted with a few isolated cumuliforms. In reality, though, it must have been deep night, for it was certainly early morning when we lurched back from the photograph fields only a few hours later. Sarah spent most of the walk talking about an exotic form of postal system, and by the time we got to the tower entrance, after two short detours to avoid policemen seeking out errant drinkers, she'd managed to outline everything, from the permissible package sizes to the particular pejoratives of sorting room disputes. I was enthralled.

"When a runner trips on a stamp captain's stool, he'll likely declare the captain a *perfopod*, unless the stamp captain has a red sash. In that case, the runner will cry, 'postal penalty!' and knock all of the captain's envelopes to the floor. Remember, those letters which touch sawdust will have to be resterilized."

The door of the Tisholong Bridge guardhouse was a sturdy, decorated slab of green metal with no recognizable handle. It was very slightly ajar, and we managed to pull it open by grasping the head of a figure on the centermost frieze. After passing through, we found ourselves in a pleasant, windowed room overlooking the river. A wide table stood in the middle of the room, and desks with radio equipment ran around the edges. The entire floor was piled high with cigarette butts. I was peering down the dark spiral staircase when I heard Sarah stifle a scream behind me. Turning, I noticed that a man was reclined in a chair with his big-booted feet up on the table and an extinguished cigarette stuck in the corner of this mouth. Gratefully, we discovered that he was asleep. Sarah wanted to put some of the drink under his nose as a prank, but I, apparently less intoxicated although I was feeling it rather strongly, guided her down the staircase in silence.

We'd brought no light, so the descent was accomplished entirely by feel and gravity in a half-tumble. Down below us, we heard murmuring which developed, as we crashed down the stairs, into the mysterious sound of far-off conversations. Eventually we began to see faint outlines of the steps and railings, and I realized that we were about to spill out into the photographs.

"Sarah," I whispered. "Be cautious."

"I think I know who they are! I recognize their gibber."

It took me a minute to realize who she was referring to, and by that time we were at the bottom and gazing out over the chiaroscuro of rolling picture hills, lit by the distant, isolated streetlight. Silhouetted at its base was a group of rocking figures, the sound of their unbreaking chatter faintly echoing off the unseen cavernous walls.

"Those people are the yarn people?" I asked.

"The Manifesto Multitude, the Landfill League, the Entangled Imbibers," she answered as she stared off in wonder at the landscape.

"I don't think I like them."

"They're lovely people."

"They torment Grel!"

"Grel needs tormenting."

With encouragement from Sarah, I took a deep swig from my milk bottle, and soon, enthusiastic curiosity drowned out my apprehension. I felt myself walking toward the group with Sarah at my side exclaiming wildly about the pictures she saw at her feet. There were sleighs of blanket-draped revelers, industrial cashew processing lines, advanced helicopters without landing gear, stacks of empty ice cream cones, construction workers on a dull vacation, and tottering piles of confiscated weaponry. As we walked, Sarah picked up her favorites and put them in her coat pockets—she told me that she wanted to use them for an art project. And then before I had time to stop and reconsider, we stepped into the illuminated cone of the streetlight. Immediately, the strange people noticed us and pointed and cackled until I felt small and miserable. I turned to run but tripped over a length of nylon cord and crashed into a pile of lumber raft details. Sarah pulled me to my feet, and we found ourselves propelled by sluggish hands into the center of the rabble.

I was bombarded by color and noise from every direction, and although I could tell I was being addressed, I couldn't focus on any one voice. A man before me, adorned in a patchwork of takeout boxes, was motioning for me to do something I couldn't interpret. To his left was a dancing woman wearing a reflective orange construction barrel through which she'd cut holes for her arms and head. I felt a push from behind and whirled around to see a set of twins in a single, very large sweater eagerly encircling my ankle with nylon string. Kicking free, I fought my way through the sea of gesturing limbs in search of Sarah but only glimpsed her through stomping legs and oscillating necks. Everywhere I turned, hands reached toward me, caught up the loose ends of my clothing, stroking me. The hands looked sickly, as if their owners suffered from chicken pox, but the sores unnaturally throbbed in color. How was that happening? I tried to see if other colors were changing, but everything moved too quickly. Desperately, I tore off the hem of someone's neon vest and held it up before my eyes. It was polka-dotted red on green, then it changed to orange on blue, then to yellow on violet. I looked up at the streetlight and made sure that no one was tampering with it to manufacture my optical crisis.

"The spots!" I cried in terror. "Sarah, I'm seeing the spots!"

I closed my eyes but the colors came with me and occupied the darkness. Outside, I could hear my frantic voice still shouting, while inside, I spoke to myself calmly and rationally about subjects that were disconnected from any comprehensible reality. The hands lowered me gently to the ground, and I felt the cool touch of the streetlight's post on my forearm.

"Pinson Charfo," said an immaculate voice very close to my ear. "I'm glad to finally meet you."

I cast my eyes around behind my lids, looking between the colorful spots for the source, and finally convinced myself that the voice was not so close to my ear that it was inside of it.

"I'm pleased to meet—" I began but was cut off by the lip of a glass bottle put to my mouth.

Spluttering in protest, I eventually came to realize that it wasn't the milk bottle, but quinine. The bitter juice tasted sweet compared to what I'd filled myself with earlier, and I sucked it down with sincerity until an unseen hand took it away.

"I'm pleased to ..." but I gave up and started in a more honest direction. "I'd love to meet you, but I'm having trouble getting out from inside my head."

Afterward, I wasn't sure if I'd said any of that aloud, since I hadn't heard my own voice; in my experience, my words generally came back around to my ears when I was done saying them, and I was usually able to hear them in my mind, delayed a little behind my current line of thought. I tried saying it all again and listened very closely, but I still didn't hear any sound. Had the quinine made me deaf or mute? I struggled in frustration, on the ground among the prints, but only managed to strike my head on the lamppost. The collision filled my head with flashes of light, and this, in turn, made me aware of the fact that the spots were no longer present. It was a comforting realization and calmed me down a little.

"I'd love to meet you, but I'm having trouble getting out from inside my head," I attempted for the third time.

I heard myself then, very faintly from behind the silence. It wasn't silence, I finally came to understand, but the unending drone of the wild people around me.

"Pin," came Sarah's voice. "Stop interrupting."

"I'm just trying to make sure I'm not dead."

"That's admirable," answered the clean voice of the man I hadn't yet met.

"Well, can you see anything?" Sarah asked.

I opened my eyes, astonished at the ease of the maneuver. Before me, on short towers of sturdy prints, sat Sarah and Sefting Cormill; it took me no time at all to recognize the dark-skinned, white-haired gentleman I'd gazed at for hours the night before in my sleep.

Mr. Cormill was saying something, but I excitedly interrupted him. "You're real! Oh, I'm so glad it's you and not the other one."

He stopped speaking and expressed amused confusion. Mr. Cormill was dressed up like one of the oppressive lunatics, with postcard leggings and a backpack shirt, but he carried his signature polka-dotted suitcase, balancing it demurely on his sharp knees. A number of nylon strands ran from his ankles and wrists, off into the crowd.

"Bruth, I mean. I'm so glad you're not Bruth," I clarified.

"Bruth? I'm also terribly pleased I'm not Bruth. What a hideous name."

"But he has your name, too! He's Bruth Cormill."

"A seriously unfortunate development," he replied with a hint of genuine displeasure.

Sarah kept gazing up into the light above us and nodding to some inaudible beat; she was quite clearly intoxicated, but the healthy kind that only warranted embraces.

"Bruth Cormill has a really big wrench," I added and illustrated with my arms.

"That is remarkable and impressive. Does he work in an electric plant?"

"He's an auto mechanic with a jumpsuit and a nametag."

"Pin, let Mr. Cormill talk about his city," Sarah broke in.

I waved my hand in apology and leaned back against the streetlight. The crowd around us was chanting something, but we ignored it.

"My city is a protest city. It's going to be the first one ever constructed. Are you familiar with the concept of a protest city?"

Sarah answered, "No, I've never heard of it," at the same moment that I replied, "I really am sorry to have interrupted, and to have been so out of touch with reality a moment ago."

They both looked at me. I apologized again, so they would know I meant it.

"My guess," continued Sarah, "is that it's a city built in order to protest some sinister policy."

Meanwhile, I held up my right hand and shook it to indicate that I preferred to refrain from sharing my guess and also to demonstrate that I confidently rode the current of drink.

"The protest city idea was first formulated by two prominent philosophers in an exchange of letters. I won't name the philosophers because I think it could unfairly affect your opinion of the idea. They aren't vile philosophers, nothing like that, but it's not polite to the idea if we give it too many associations before we think a little bit about it."

I liked Mr. Cormill's style; he was very proper and spoke in the most compassionate way I'd ever heard anyone speak. His beliefs with respect to authorial intent also rang true for me, though I was naturally disposed toward any ideology involving rejection.

"A protest city is designed in such a way that whichever street one walks down, one must walk in the midst of a protest. The protests are the traditional sort, involving banners, megaphones, and sometimes little acts of vandalism. Their intention is to cause such a respectful nuisance that their message is both broadcast and appreciated. In their correspondence, the two philosophers debate the logistics of protest cities extensively. In my city's design, I side more with . . ." Mr. Cormill chuckled, "the leftmost one. Hm. That's bad because of the political connotations. The *northernmost one*, perhaps, is better. In any case, we will call him Alice and the other one, my opposition, Bob. I'll refer to them both as males, but that's for ease and not in order to indicate any truth about their sex or gender. On that note, I'm only distinguishing between sex and gender because I was taught correctly. In actuality, I reject gender in favor of personality."

To my satisfaction, he was rejecting again, and I was compelled to give Mr. Cormill a high five; his hand was dry and rough, and I drew mine back quickly because it seemed a very childish hand by comparison. Sarah was playing a finger game with one of the babblers but occasionally nodded at Mr. Cormill to indicate that she was listening. I didn't yet feel up to any serious multitasking, so I just dug my feet around in the photographs to make uninteresting shapes.

"In one early letter, Bob points out to Alice that since disruption is an important part of protesting, care must be taken in the city's design to include people and activities to disrupt. Excluding protesters, who in their right mind would spend time in a city where every avenue is filled with a protest? Bob offered the following crude solution: invite a great number of workers to come to the city, but arrange everything in such a way that the cheap housing they're offered is on one side of the city, and the good-paying jobs in the new factories are on the other side. These new citizens would be forced to commute through the protests every day, but their desirable lives wouldn't be so inconvenienced that they'd decide to move away. Of course, Bob adds, a number of checks would have to be worked out in order to prevent these people from moving closer to the factories or building big roundabout expressways. Alice rightly criticizes that this could only end in disaster, such as class warfare or maybe even implosion."

"Implosion?" I asked.

"Ah, sorry, it's a technical term. If a significant number of protesters get fed up with supporting their cause and abandon their protest, then their assigned streets would free up and everyone would travel by way of these empty streets in order to avoid protests. Suddenly protesters would drop in number, because, you see, most protesters are just people trying to get from A to B, and the city would cease to be a protest city."

"But if you become a protester just by going from A

to B, how do you keep your disrupted citizens, the ones with nice houses and factory jobs, from becoming protesters?"

"Alice posed that very question to Bob. He devised a solution involving a system of tunnels underneath the city for the workers to travel through. These tunnels would be filled with paint cannons that shoot out quantities of different colored paint proportional to the number of protesters in the corresponding protests. It's a ridiculous solution. A number of papers support Bob by claiming it was simply a convenient example to prove the existence of a workable system. In my opinion, though, Bob really thinks that paint cannons are the best solution."

"Honestly," said Sarah, "the whole concept is ridiculous. Why would anyone want to build, or even think about, a protest city in the first place?"

"That's a difficult question to answer, because although there are a number of good reasons, most proponents are drawn to the idea by a little tickle of their aesthetics."

"What's one of the good reasons?" Sarah answered, unconvinced.

"Many people want to change the world, but not

many are willing to go very far out of their way to do it. Living in a protest city, you protest every day, even when you're just going out to buy milk."

"I could see that reason from the start, but it isn't a good one. If a person wants to protest but is too lazy to do it, they'd be way too lazy to move to a protest city."

"You're right. In fact, Alice and Bob argue about the best way to garner city residents. In the end, Bob supports both adoption and enticing people in by way of extremely good public services while Alice advocates recruiting movements en masse to establish districts with lots of flags and code words."

"So, what's one of the good reasons that's actually good?" Sarah pushed.

"In a protest city, one may change one's principles simply by walking down a different street. If one wants to experiment with new beliefs, one can simply turn left instead of right."

"But I want to know how Alice solves the disruption problem you were talking about before," I interrupted.

"Alice suggests that the city streets can be laid out in such a way that the protests disrupt other protests. It's very simple," Mr. Cormill replied.

Suddenly, a tide of the wild people hit Sarah. She toppled forward from her photograph seat. I jumped to my feet to help her up before she was trampled. I felt limber and rejuvenated; from experience, I knew that this feeling meant I was feeding off of my final reserves of energy. It must have been tremendously late at night. The crowd had grown during our conversation, and each of its members seemed to want to be the closest to the lamppost.

"It's time to make our escape," advised Mr. Cormill. "In a few minutes we won't be able to get out."

Together, we pushed over a big, shirtless man in aluminum can pants and battled our way down the avenue he'd cleared behind him. Hands grabbed at our coats and hair, but we slapped them away. The entire place stank terribly of their drink, and it was evident that very few of the manifesto people were anything less than wildly inebriated.

Over the roar of their chatter, Sarah shouted to Mr. Cormill, "How can you run so quickly with your nylon strings?"

"It's a scam," he shouted back and held up a handful of loose ends of nylon cord. "I'm only pretending to be one of them."

"Why would you do that?"

"I'm very interested in their manifesto and think their movement would be a great one to have in my protest city. I'm doing research, if you will. I'm extremely impressed by your work, Pinson."

"My work?"

"Yes, your manifesto really has something right. I'd love to talk about it in depth sometime," he yelled, bludgeoning his way past two women wrapped in tattered parachutes. "Maybe we can chat tomorrow at Tomthy's."

"You're going to Tomthy's party?"

"Of course! I'm going as a wizard," he shouted in my ear. "I'm looking forward to seeing you plane Bernsy on that plagiarism accusation."

"But I didn't write it!" I cried. "Nor did I plagiarize it, nor have I even seen the thing."

Mr. Cormill only smiled back. The crowd had thinned out and we were now able to make our way without being accosted. Mr. Cormill abruptly stopped.

"I'm going to leave you two here. I have a few more observations to make before I go to bed," he said.

"Well, I can think of little else besides bed," I said. "But before I go, Mr. Cormill, what does Ralfo have to do with all this?"

"Ralfo?" he asked, suspiciously.

"I found a letter from him, to you, in my bed."

"That's curious. He's a dangerous man. My advice is to stay clear of him. Ralfo has been fighting me and my city every step of the way. He's a shrewd businessman and has amassed a fortune selling family foods, so he has the resources to meddle significantly."

With that, Mr. Cormill turned and dove back into the crowd, slicing his way through with his polka-dotted suitcase.

*

I do not remember very clearly how we got home. When I awoke in my bed with no sign of Sarah, it was in one of those miserable ways. I couldn't see anything because of rheum—had I been crying?—and sweat held everything in my bed together in a disgusting mass. The air was hot and muggy because I'd left the windows open, and it was already past noon. I could smell my shoes from across the room. My body was unresponsive, so I screamed until I managed to roll out onto the floor.

Outside, I could hear the roar of the city; it didn't

seem to be missing me. Together, we gave the city life, but the city would not die or even feel sick unless a lot of us did, and maybe not even then. With our personalities and our self-love, we created something with its own personality and self-love. It would've been so much better to have made something unlike us, something that would deeply care if any single one of us disappeared.

Down on the floor, it was less hot, but when my sluggish fingers finally chipped my lids open, I was afforded a view of the space beneath my bed, which was not a pleasant place. With the help of my chair, I clambered to my feet and glared around my room. The offensive smell of my shoes came to my nostrils again. It wasn't a particularly bad smell—I hadn't done anything special to them—but it was intolerable to me somehow, and without restraint, I picked my shoes up by the laces and flung them out through the window. Almost immediately, I heard a cry of surprise.

"The Pin hangs over?" Mrs. Fiss called from below.

Being addressed renewed my humor. Communication had a mysterious restorative power which I often neglected, perhaps more consciously than I wanted to admit. I felt that maybe I'd been too pessimistic about the city. It kept going on without me while I slept, but the whole time it'd remembered I was curled up in my room and hadn't done anything to disturb me. As a child, I'd sometimes fall asleep while on errands with my parents, and when we returned home, my mother would leave me out in the car, asleep. What they felt toward me wasn't carelessness, as I once assumed; instead, it was a very definite form of love. The city loved me in the same way.

"Sorry, Mrs. Fiss. It's that madness we get," I apologized, looking down from my room.

Mrs. Fiss had company and had laid out a little picnic on the stairs. Everyone was well-dressed. My shoes lay very near to the teapot but appeared to have caused no damage.

"The terror?"

I nodded. Mrs. Fiss's guests looked up at me with curiosity and whispered amongst themselves.

"I'll just keep them here for you, for when you need them later," said Mrs. Fiss as she gestured at my footwear.

"Thank you, Mrs. Fiss. I'll be down soon."

I pulled my head into my room and prepared myself for what was left of the day. It was only after I'd put my socks on that I noticed, camouflaged by the creases in my bedspread, a crumpled note which read as follows.

Dearest Meesquich,

Deep,, inside my, chest I feel a PAIN,. It feels, like, it's going to ,EXPLODE. Explode,, like a stick of DYNAMITE in the ASS of a steer. You treated me, NASTY.

Next time we pass on the sidewalk, you look LEFT, and I'll look RIGHT. That way, our eyes won't see each other.

You committed an act of treachery when you came to me last. I know you lied to me. You took credit for a note that I, myself, had written. You see, Charfo, you are accused of plagiarizing Bernsy's manifesto. I had to discover empirically—I might be fat, but I respect science immensely—whether or not that was the case. I secreted a note into your sheets, and the next day you came to me and demonstrated quite clearly that you have the mind of a villain—you and Cormill both. I suspected you two were working together, and after your lie, I'm sure of it. Because of your act of treachery I'm going to get mad and set something on fire. I'll let you guess what.

Take a look in this morning's paper, the Charfo Column.
You'll find a little treat there.

Sincerely,

Peter Ralfo Sr.

I rushed to my door and found the day's paper on top of the heap of others that I'd never bothered to look at and, in the way every writer can, flipped to my column in an instant. What I found there was something very unexpected and troubling.

You won't be able to go to the racetrack today, after all. You dearly want to feel dejected about it but you capably recognize that it's you who's the party at fault. You can't possibly feel dejected without adding to it a heap of guilt—you already have plenty of that stuff at your fingertips, and it's better to not let it reach critical mass. Yesterday, honestly, you could have been more dutiful and done what needed to be done before it needed to be done today. Or, you could have not stayed up so late last night thinking about women. What you're feeling this morning is what you call enigmatic pain, which, you admit, is the euphemism you've concocted to describe the sensation you get when you look up and realize that you are definitively inadequate for valuable existence and, simultaneously, that your perpetual hangover has become noticeably worse.

Your name is Pinson Charfo, but you prefer to just go by Charfo because you love the way it sounds. This is your column and today you have just enough time to topple from your bed, claw your way up to your desk, and compose this particular piece before your deadline buckles under the pressure. You handily accomplish the first two tasks—a sure sign of habit—but you become puzzled and indecisive the instant you finally put the tip of your pen to the crisp paper.

"What do I do now?"

We don't answer you, so you uncertainly begin to draw a spiral. You're careful to do it over in a corner, not in order to preserve your writing space, but because you feel more comfortable doing it over there where someone is less likely to notice it. But you've started on the outside and gone inward, which leads to a rising disillusionment as you internalize the fact that this little form of procrastination cannot possibly continue forever. You start again in another corner, starting from the inside this time, but run off the page due to bad planning.

"I really am hopeless at writing."

You're not the sort of person who's prone to delusions, but perhaps that's because of simplemindedness. When your employer talks to you, he tells you plenty of things you didn't know, and you nod a lot and act aloof in order to seem like you have a reasonable intellect. Now you're rocking back and forth in your chair. Something is bothering you, and the motion helps you to identify it: you can't write when someone else is looking.

"I can't write when you're looking."

"We're not looking. Don't worry," we reply.

We are looking, though. You've started to draw little triangles in a row at the bottom of the page. One particular triangle is very large and one side of it is quite obviously curved. Another has an embarrassingly sloppy vertex.

"Your eyes are open and you're looking right at where my hands are," you protest.

"We're daydreaming. Don't worry."

"It still makes me uncomfortable."

"What if we prove that we can't see what you're doing?"

"I suppose that might make me feel better," you answer.

Your nose has begun to run, but you don't seem to notice.

"How about you write down a word, then we'll guess what it is. If we're right, we're obviously able to see what you write, but if we're wrong, then you can feel secure."

"That's a good idea!" you exclaim.

This is just the sort of scam you'd fall for. On the paper you write testimony.

"Are you ready?" we ask, feigning blindness.

"Yes. Can you see what I've written?"

"You've written fossil."

"No, I've written testimony!" you exclaim. "One more, just to be safe."

"We're ready when you are."

"Okay, what have I written?"

"You've written catastrophe."

"Ha!" you cheer. "It was pumice. Well, I certainly feel much better."

"We're very happy to help. Now, don't miss your deadline. You don't have much time left," we warn.

You become very serious and hunch over the paper. After a minute or so of miming, you quickly glance up at us, then again. You wave at us but we don't fall for it. Believing wholeheartedly that we're daydreaming and not watching your every move, you quietly slide open the drawer in your desk and take out two large volumes. The first appears to be a collection of old and obscure newspaper articles while the second is an enormous thesaurus. You flip randomly to a page in the first volume and start copying the words out onto the paper before you. Every once in a while you look up one of the words in the thesaurus and write down a synonym instead; you believe this will shield your duplicity.

We can't take it anymore and clear our throats; injustice must be swatted. You jump and turn very slowly to see that we've raised our hands threateningly and put on extremely stern expressions.

"Oh! But this isn't what it looks like," you protest.

"We've always suspected you were a cheat, didn't we?" We all nod together.

"It's just a simple exercise! I loosen my wrist by copying this way. Otherwise I get cramps halfway through and have to send for ice."

We ignore your pathetics and take turns flipping through your volume of articles until each of us has independently verified that you're a thieving scamp.

"Here's the one about healing competitions: 'The contestants are arranged in a row and a certified doctor patiently traverses the line, applying precision wounds of perfect uniformity to each outstretched arm.' In Charfo's column, he swapped out a few different words. Charfo's doctor didn't hurt the competitor's arms, but their legs.

"And it wasn't certified doctors, but official ones. Charfo should have stuck with certified. It's much better."

You blather, and we glare.

"The only thing for you to do now is to apologize and then to flee before the mobs come."

You continue to blather, and we continue to glare.

"Should we strike him?" the most enthusiastic one among us suggests.

"Okay, okay! Let me have my say and then I'll be off," you cry.

"But do it without any of your usual nonsense. Be frank with it. We've already gone right past the end of your column and are halfway through the space allocated for the humorous foreign correspondents. We don't want to make the humorous foreign correspondents angry."

You clear your throat and wipe your nose with the back of your hand.

In a shaky voice, you say, "Every night, I wake up very nearly always at two o'clock because of a pain in my ankles. As a consequence, I dream quite vividly and sometimes cry out because of the unpleasant things I experience. I compulsively sweep, often for more than three hours of the day. When the broom is in my hand, I don't think of anything other than the little bits of dirt I find. I get very excited over small piles of sand; I admit, I sometimes hide them around the feet of my furniture beforehand, just to make it all the more enjoyable. As a child, some of my teeth never fell out. They're still in my mouth, underdeveloped and unsuitable to a mature appetite. I find it very pleasurable to rub my eyes, even though doing so makes them itch intolerably. I inconsistently switch between uppercase and lowercase, often in a single word. These are the qualities that best define my character. I plagiarize. It's true. I'm sorry for it, but I can't do otherwise because the character that binds me has certain inviolate conclusions. I plagiarize, and I don't like the taste of water. I'm sorry about both of these qualities, in equal measure. I'll endeavor to improve them. I'm resigned to pursue the necessary struggle."

We do not accept your apology; we all agree that it's a very bad one.

I stood very still and let the room spin quietly around my head. Ralfo had somehow managed to replace my real column with one in which I confess to being a plagiarist. Aside from the obvious wave of libel, this new column had two worrying undercurrents. First, it elicited some kind of response from me. To stay on course and quietly take responsibility for this column would be, in effect, to acquiesce to the charges, to actually adopt the fictional role of scoundrel as my own true role. Second, the column demonstrated that Ralfo had a frightening cunning. And not only had he swapped in his own work, but he'd managed to access my bed while I slept, in order to deposit the note. The note itself revealed more trouble. It meant Carolina was not real, which meant, further, that my encounter with Ralfo, as Mr. Cormill warned, had been rife with treachery.

But what should I do? And, also importantly, what would Ralfo light on fire? He hadn't set fire to my room, but how about Sarah's? I immediately ran down a floor and found no sign of conflagration. I pounded on her door, but she didn't seem to be home. Had Ralfo set Sarah on fire? I needed Grel. What if Grel were on fire? In an instant I was downstairs and struggling to put on my shoes despite the shaking of my hands.

Only after I'd tied them and looked up did I realize that Sarah was there and that Mrs. Fiss had been trying to tell me something for some time.

"Pin, dear, Grel sent one of his ruffians over to say

that he'd meet you at Tomthy's," she repeated when she could see I was finally listening. "He says he'll be dressed as a wizard."

"But we were supposed to have dinner!" I cried.

"You wouldn't have time for it anyway," Sarah pointed out. "You have to get ready, then we'll take a cab out to Tomthy's estate. Get a book for the ride."

It was true. I had just enough time to go upstairs, wash the infragrant sweat from under my arms, pick up my costume across town at Mr. Evesong's, and stop at a cafe to prime myself for the party before we took the long trip to Tomthy's. It was odd, I admitted, to still go to the party. After Ralfo's reveal, I had much bigger problems to deal with. But as I still had no course of action to resolve any of these problems, without the party I would've simply suffered around the city until I collapsed somewhere.

"I have to get my costume still," I told Sarah. "And I'm in dire need of a coffee."

"I got you a costume," Sarah replied petulantly.

"I don't want to be a wizard, Sarah. I'm going as a deer hunter. I have to go to Mr. Evesong's shop."

She opened her mouth to object; I continued talking

in order to prevent her. "Have you read my column today?"

Sarah shook her head and Mrs. Fiss looked at the ground. I began to summarize it, but, hesitantly, one of Mrs. Fiss's guests raised her gloved hand.

"Oh, I read that," she announced.

I pointed at her.

"The point is that I didn't write it. Peter Ralfo Sr. wrote it, and he's after me. He even intends to light something on fire."

Everyone began to ask for details all at once, but I told them I didn't know anything.

Sarah clearly saw that I was overwhelmed and guided me back into the building. I went up to my room and washed the previous night off my skin. Afterward, I sat on the toilet and repeatedly reread Ralfo's column until I realized my eyes were focused past the paper. There was a tremor in my thigh. I threw the newspaper into a corner and washed myself again. By the time I was back outside, the afternoon sun had already begun to descend, and Mrs. Fiss and her guests were gone.

My desperate outlook convinced me to make the coffee stop before the costume stop. I ordered the most expensive cup at a bustling counter. Throughout the crowded cafe, patrons held the daily paper in front of their faces, as strangers do in spy movies. I could only imagine they were greedily reading my hijacked column. Though the newspaper never included a photograph of me, I still felt conspicuous and alone; I resolved that I'd tell Sarah all about the Ralfo mystery on the way to Tomthy's.

A bright-cheeked postal worker at a nearby table put down his paper and said to me, "Have you read this unusual piece today?"

"Yes," I replied dismissively.

"What do you make of the idea?" he pushed.

"I found it hurtful. Charfo must have a ghostwriter this week."

"Charfo? What position does he play? Those idiots are always padding out the roster with useless rookies."

I paid my bill and walked unsteadily out to the street.

Mr. Evesong was closing his shop a few minutes early when I arrived, and he expressed sincere relief that I'd arrived before he left. The costume he'd made for me was wonderfully detailed, and the buckskins' fringe was elegant in that way only something anachronistic can be. My enthusiasm regarding the product of his labor encouraged Mr. Evesong to give me a long-winded tour of his inventory. I spent the time nodding and touching various fabrics, trying not to recall the words of Ralfo I'd read over and over in my bathroom. Mr. Evesong concluded by showing me his most prized work: a frightening tapir-warrior suit he'd made for the Grenswopp film, which had been canceled a year ago. From inside, the wearer could control the mask's lips with unsettling precision. Mr. Evesong demonstrated this feature to me. I quoted a relevant line from the game. This new encouragement led to a string of quotes and references I barely kept up with until I told him I had to be somewhere.

On my way out, my costume packaged neatly under my arm, I conspiratorially asked Mr. Evesong if he had any rolls of nylon cord. Unfortunately, he told me, earnestly taking his wire glasses off, all of the nylon cord had sold out.

*

Tomthy Schream Illstington-Fo was the city's contact in the colorful world of aristocracy. For thirty years, Tomthy ruled a prosperous little seaside country replete with militarism, monuments, and taxes. He ruled by the authority of a five-hundred-year bloodline of kings, many of whom had been functionally mindsick—for example, King Schream IX had made death illegal and punishable by exile. But a decade ago, Tomthy became absentminded and lost his throne to an amputee general with an ingeniously designed electric pistol. Afterward, there were purges, naturally, which meant soaring exile rates. Tomthy escaped through a series of tunnels his predecessors—and honestly, Tomthy himself—used in order to sneak prostitutes into the palace from the neighboring nation, where the practice wasn't punishable by diseasing. After a couple of years of cruising the gilded byways of international society, Tomthy arrived in our city and bought an enormous estate with very questionably obtained funds. The man held a number of balls for the privileged throughout the year, but in August, he always hosted a costume party for students and artists. Of course, following the natural order of things, these lowly costume parties became the most anticipated event, and all the privileged felt compelled to appear as well.

When Sarah and I stepped from our cab, we found to our delight that Tomthy had arranged for the party to be held in his extensive hedge maze. It was decorated in a foreign style, with live-flame lanterns adorning the tops of every bush and a fleet of illuminating blimps floating overhead. Excited revelers were trooping through the entryway. It was a beautiful, clear night, and marvelous fireflies hovered everywhere but never settled on anything.

"There are people with binoculars in those blimps," Sarah observed.

"Sarah, everyone here is dressed as a wizard."

"Yes, of course they are," she replied. "The invitation asked them to do that."

"Well, I guess I understand your insistence, now."

"You didn't ever read your invitation?"

"No, I threw it into some corner. I wasn't going to go, but then you asked me to."

Sarah caught me under the arm and lead me toward the entrance. She grinned madly and told an anecdote about the last time she'd been in a maze.

"Sarah, I told you I'd end up making a scene," I interrupted, the embarrassment of my appearance settling in.

I assessed my costume from above. It was possible to interpret it as some kind of exotic wizard if I kept the rifle hidden under my fringe. There were all sorts of wizards, and plus, I wormed, a wizard could easily change form into whatever shape he wanted; there was certainly a famous wizard who'd disguised himself as a deer hunter at some point in history.

She laughed at me.

"Don't worry about it! I didn't want you to go as a wizard, anyway. I knew you wouldn't if I bugged you about it."

"What if they don't let me in?" I waved wildly around me. "They're all wizards! What if I push my hat up from the inside, like this? Is it taller?"

"You're Pinson Charfo."

"I am?"

"Aren't you?"

"Yes."

"Since when did you worry about this sort of thing?"

She walked through the entrance, past a squad of short people dressed as goblin soldiers. They simply nodded as I ran through the green archway after her.

"Since someone else started being me," I answered.

Sarah took two test tubes from the tray of a nearby goblin and drained one while passing the other to me. It was strong punch. I looked in the bottom of the empty tube but didn't find any misplaced objects.

"You mean the manifesto?"

"Yes. Whoever the author is, he stole Bernsy's piece and used my name. That's what set this whole mess in motion. And I don't think it's Ralfo, because he said he instigated all of his intrigue in order to find out if I were a plagiarist. But that leaves a lot of people to be suspicious of, considering the population of the world."

We made a few random turns through the maze and found ourselves in a small grassy opening. Groups of partygoers stood in little circles, chatting and marveling at the fireflies.

"These wizards must be uninteresting," Sarah announced. "Why would they settle down here, right at the beginning?"

"Maybe they're just getting organized."

Sarah nodded her head thoughtfully. "You could be right. That one in the floppy scholastic hat seems very disorganized."

The wizard Sarah pointed out stood to the side of one of the larger groups. He wore a long dark cloak decorated with outlandish creatures eating one another and themselves. It was unclear if his hat was supposed to be that squashed and lopsided or if he'd simply mangled it on the way to the party. On one foot he wore a tennis shoe, while on the other he wore a curled-toe slipper. He was frantically running his hands through all of his many wizard pockets.

"Actually, I know that one," I said.

"He seems your type."

"It's Ret Sharing, the hobbyist."

I brought Sarah over to the man, who didn't look up until I poked him rather aggressively in the sternum. Sarah and Ret each did their best to express how pleased they were to make the acquaintance of the other, but the pleasantries quickly lulled, for Ret was immersed in his frenetic search, and Sarah kept glancing greedily down the various corridors leading further into the maze.

"Ret, I can't help but notice you're looking for something."

"It's my other slipper," he mumbled. "I forgot to put them on before coming and just now started changing into them, but I was also taking note of the lightning bugs, and things got lost or mixed-up, and now I can't find the next slipper to put on, nor the sneaker I just took off."

"At least you have something to wear on each foot," I consoled.

Our calm in the face of a trial that he rated immensely troubling evidently comforted him. Ret became visibly more relaxed and shrugged his shoulders.

"This sort of thing seems to happen to me quite often. I'm beginning to think Nature is using her trickery to get back at me for all of the observations I've made of her over the years. For example, I became aware of my missing slipper just seconds after making the important discovery that it was far too damp in the air for these lampyrids to be making their flashes through any electrical means. In some ways it's gratifying, for it must have been a very accurate observation in order for her to feel pained enough to steal my footwear."

Sarah's impatience seized command; she dragged me away. I invited Ret to come along, but he quickly fell behind as he hobbied over every little detail. We soon lost him in the windings, but we happily told ourselves that he probably hadn't noticed our disappearance or even, Sarah remarked, our presence in the first place.

At intersections, we turned without thought, too excited over presenting ourselves to the wonders of the maze to take any exploratory precautions. We came across clearings where music was played by orchestras dressed as enormous crickets and wizards filled the dance floors; we crossed rivers that ran between the hedges and were navigated by small, goblin-powered gondolas; we uncovered entrances to secret shortcuts, hidden behind modernist statues and punch waterfalls; we collected scraps of maps from theatrically lit pedestals and wizened goblins who only spoke in riddles; we set off fireworks which burst into the most enigmatic shapes until one happened to orient in just the right way so that we saw that it portrayed the Tisholong Bridge. Yet we still hadn't found the end of the maze, nor, again, the beginning, nor, to our dismay, Grel.

We resolved to focus and began to diligently record our route in Sarah's prop spellbook. From time to time, we passed through a section of the maze depicted on the map fragments we'd found, and when we came across wizards who weren't staggering more than us, we carefully compared notes, making sure to not reveal our most promising lore. We found fewer and fewer wizards on our route, and eventually we trekked for half-hour stretches without seeing anyone other than ourselves. The pathways were overgrown with weeds, and we were forced to brush away errant branches from the unkempt hedges on either side, which often rose so high that they bent over and met above our heads.

When we came to an opening with a ruined wooden structure in the middle, Sarah and I took a moment to rest on the grass under the peaceful light of a blimp. She lay on her back and told me the story of when she was little and her father had found a cockroach in the sugar pot while on the patio of a restaurant. The waitress, not believing Sarah's father, had examined the sugar for herself, and in her shock at finding what she really should have expected to see there, the waitress catapulted the creature into the air with the spoon. The unfortunate insect landed in Sarah's brother's astonished mouth, and he turned and emptied his stomach's contents into a potted plant. Even before finishing, the brother was asking repeatedly if the cockroach had come out. The only person with the courage to look had been Sarah. She told him that the cockroach was nowhere to be seen, while, truthfully, she had watched it scramble away into the sewer. Her brother didn't eat for a week afterward, asserting that he needed to reserve all of his digestive powers for the destruction of the intruder.

"I ask that you turn your conversation in a more erudite direction," came a sharp voice from behind us. "My daughter's coming along shortly."

I rocketed to my feet, while Sarah rolled over onto her stomach, to see a short and wide wizard in blue garb from head to toe. Above his two-foot-long indigo slippers and perfectly tailored navy robe, and beneath his comically small hat which resembled a blueberry jelly, he even wore cerulean dye in his mustache and beard.

It was Mavil's father, my employer, and he recognized me at the same instant.

"Charfo," he said with unmasked disappointment. "Here?"

"I find it useful to study society on the rare occasion," I lied.

My hands adopted their routine of pocket shuffling in spite of my mind's quick realization that the prints I'd collected hadn't been transferred to my buckskins.

"I see," he replied, indicating Sarah with displeasure. "No more of that filth. My daughter is here."

Mavil came out from a behind a hedge and curtsied when she saw me. With bright blonde hair, a cheerful little face, and an energy in her movement that gave one the impression that she would fly fifty feet with each step—had she not been tempering the impulse with a mischievous grace—it would have been hard to dress her in anything very wizardy. So, she wore a simple white dress and a pair of translucent wings, becoming the image of a very tasteful sprite.

"I'm a sprite!" she announced superfluously. "But often people call me a fairy. Are they wrong? Or is *sprite* another one of those foreign words we find in poems?"

"You're a sprite," her father answered unhelpfully.

"Sprites comprise a more general clade of fantastic creature. Fairies are sprites, but sprites aren't all fairies," I answered. "For example, some elf species are sprites, too."

"You're not following the curriculum," her father remarked with displeasure.

"I'm sorry."

"But it's quite mathematical, a good example of set theory," came Sarah to my rescue.

"Is set theory suitably abstract?"

"Yes, certainly," I quickly replied.

Mavil's father produced a reluctant sound of approval.

He then turned to his daughter. "Now, back to the lesson."

Mavil took a small notebook from a pocket on the side of her skirt, opened it, and read, "'Mrs. Welfire, how do you do?' 'I do well and good, most certainly, and you?'

'I do most certainly well and good, too.' 'Mrs. Trenfoddle, did I see you at the theater, last evening in a box?' 'Yes, I gave you the pleasure, most certainly. I wore a fox.' 'I most certainly had the pleasure, for it covered your drenched socks.'"

Her father squinted.

"Mistake. Society women do not wear socks."

"But I copied down exactly what they said, just as I heard it."

I grimaced twice, once for embarrassment and once on Mavil's behalf.

"Go back and listen again. This is the sort of language a young lady must adopt. You are not allowed to make mistakes with it."

Mavil scampered off.

Her father turned to me and commanded, "In future lessons, practice attentive listening for ten minutes."

"I fear Mavil would have suffered from attentive listening in this instance," I protested.

"Charfo, I like to think of you as an upbrought lad."

"Thank you," I replied uncertainly.

"So, do not make me think of you as a downbrought one."

"Of course," I answered, then paused for delicacy.

"But I don't think you would have approved of Mavil hearing what those society ladies actually said."

"There's no secret in my household regarding lox, Charfo."

"But I'd assume there's one regarding French pox."

"Or clenched cocks," put in Sarah.

Mavil's father took a moment to understand me. I could tell the instant he finally saw what I meant, because he produced an enormous frown and turned to track down his daughter before her ears became further befouled.

"On the subject of secrets," I called after him, "I got the photographs for you."

He stopped and turned back toward us. The blimps' lights flickered.

"What photographs?"

"The disreputable prints," I clarified.

"I didn't ask for photographs," Mavil's father replied slowly. "Charfo, this is no time for nonsense."

He turned and stalked off down a row of hedges.

I wasn't sure what to make of it. Had I blundered— he truly hadn't wanted prints after all—or was Mavil's father simply being discreet? It would have been convenient to write the reaction off as discretion, but I couldn't make it fit with the image I remembered of his confused brow throwing the rest of his face into shadow beneath the blinking lights from above.

Sarah patted me on the back.

"I guess you can keep the prints for yourself," she joked.

We resumed our journey, but in silence. I felt the pressure of the stress returning to my spine, that unaccountable feeling of something failing within me.

The air in this district was thicker than elsewhere in the maze and carried an organic scent which stifled and invigorated in sequence. With every breath, I felt as though each particle of air I sucked in took a breath of its own, and my lungs momentarily screamed out against the density, only to exclaim in exultation moments later. At my side, Sarah pinched her nose and playfully swung a stick at the vegetation hanging in our path, but I saw a dour hesitation beneath it; her upraised hand did little to cover a delicate frown, and she swung with no great force. I was reminded of Mr. Selmare's performance in the photograph shop.

We were roused from our introversions by the sound of faint whimpering from behind a nearby hedge. Using our notes, we eventually found our way to its source after winding through a field of twelve-foot grass and then through a hollowed tree trunk, with only a cloud of grumpy fireflies to light our way. On the path before us, a female wizard, on all fours, strove toward us but was restrained by something behind her. She groaned with frustration and tried to escape by sheer force, not once turning to identify the source of her imprisonment. A taut length of nylon ran from her ankle and made a sharp turn behind a hedge. She lashed out at us with her nails, but Sarah fended her off with an astrolabe from her wizard belt while I cut the cord with my hunting knife. The woman, now free, bolted off down the path without a word of acknowledgement.

"That's my glorious manifesto," I said, pointing after the wizard.

"Your glorious manifesto," Sarah replied.

We followed the nylon and increasingly came within range of a loud cacophony of expletives riding through the air above our heads.

And then, suddenly, we passed through an archway and into a wide square, paved in the old way. It was difficult to tell whether we were still in Tomthy's maze or back in the city. A heap of screaming wizards lay in the center of the square, and a number of unconcerned sheep grazed on what green things grew between the cobblestones. Each sheep had a red letter spray-painted onto it.

"I think the letters spell out *congratulations*."

A figure trotted out from behind the pile of wizards and continued in an arc around them. We watched, speechless, until the man's orbit sent him back out of view.

"Have we found the end?" Sarah asked.

Distant sounds of revelers reached our ears, but it was clear that we were far from any of the party's action. Even the blimps were elsewhere; the square was lit by a single streetlight at each of the four corners. The figure jogged back into view, but this time its course changed, and it veered toward us.

"Pin!" it cried.

It was Grel, we soon saw, in a dark robe he'd tied up above his knees to prevent it hampering his stride. I didn't know how to begin, so I just gave him a high five.

"I've caught most of them," he announced excitedly and held up a big ball of nylon string. "I've tied them up in that fountain with their own stuff!"

I saw, then, that the wizards were heaped up in the pool of a fountain which was the centerpiece of this quiet square. For an instant I thought I was back in front of Mr. Selmare's shop, but I soon saw that this fountain was slightly different. It still featured a cowled king and, though the wizards mostly obscured them, mermaids could be seen caressing his feet, but the statues were all made from roughly fitted wood which had warped from the moisture. Whoever had painted on the sheep had also seen fit to write something on the side of this fountain, but I couldn't make it out. A hundred rings of nylon held the manifesto's adherents all together in a struggling ball. A stream of water spilled out from under their mass.

"It's a good thing you made it here. Bernsy's been looking all over for you," Grel remarked, panting. "But he'll never make it. He hasn't the necessary acuity."

"Though I fear," I replied darkly, "he has an accomplice. Peter Ralfo is also after me."

"He's one of those brow-replete students? That kind we know by their nostrils, because they only attend lectures by balcony."

"Peter Ralfo is Peter Ralfo Sr. of Ralfo Family Foods. And he intends to light fire to something."

"This is not the news I'd hoped you'd bring."

"What was the news you'd hoped we'd bring?" asked Sarah.

"I'm so sleepy," Grel muttered.

A sheep painted with an L ambled over and licked his arm, but Grel didn't seem to notice. A rising whirring sound was in the air, as if all of the fireflies had decided to turn and speed toward us.

"It's in moments like these that one realizes where one has failed," he said softly.

"Where have you failed?" I asked.

"I never worked out how I'm supposed to bring my captives to Drea."

"Where is Drea?"

"At my place, reading."

The whirring was louder now and coming from somewhere in the sky. I looked up to see a blimp, dark against the stars, racing directly for us. Its windows shone with an orange light. My spine erupted, then, in a series of sharp sensations which weren't directly painful but gave the distinct impression of pain. Looking down, my eyes met Sarah, who stood before me, giving that casual salute.

"I don't want you to die in the duel with Bernsy," she said.

"I don't want to fight a duel. I'm a pacifist."

"Lots of animals don't wage war but still fight duels."

"Over honor?"

"Over whatever they like."

"What do I like?"

Sarah smiled.

At that instant, there was an enormous explosion and the blimp expanded until it filled the sky with a glowing fire that illuminated the square and silhouetted two parachuters. One was small and skeletal, kicking excitedly as he drifted to the ground; the other was portly and carrying handfuls of lanterns which he threw deliberately into the hedges. Both were shouting indistinctly behind the roar of conflagration.

"Bernsy hates you. He knows you stole that toy from him. He convinced himself that he wrote the manifesto in his sleep," Sarah said, reaching forward and grasping my shoulder.

"So, people don't actually write things in their sleep?"

"No. No one does."

She kissed me, briefly, and then turned to face the two black-robed figures who were releasing themselves from their harnesses. The big one momentarily put down his lanterns to help the little one free himself, and when he was free, he began dancing back and forth wildly. The big one resumed his lantern throwing.

"Here's your fire, Charfo!" came Ralfo's commanding voice. "You'll be steak soon enough!"

"I challenge you, Charfo!" rang the squeaky voice of the scoundrel Bernsy.

The fire in the sky was gone, but the fire around us was growing quickly and had long outshone the feeble streetlights. There was no exit other than the archway we'd first come through, not that I intended to flee; I was bolstered by Sarah's kiss, and the punch I'd steadily drained the entire night.

"I say we flee," remarked Grel, taking cover behind the sheep.

"Air your grievance, blockhead!" I shouted.

Bernsy was a short little man with rough hair and strong eyebrows that met on humid days. He was imposing, but only in the sense that you never wanted him around; it took infinite coaxing to make him leave.

"I, Bernsot Crack, son of Benjamin Crack, son of Well

Crack III, accuse you of plagiarism. You've stolen my written work and sold it for your own profit. The satisfaction I demand for your evil can only be supplied by your life."

"Bernsy the Crook, son of Bitch Crack, you wrote the stupid thing and tacked my name on it in order to ruin me with slander," I extemporized for any unseen witnesses. "Prepare to meet the fate you wish for me."

We advanced toward one another. I held my toy rifle at my hip menacingly; Bernsy was armed with something I couldn't quite make out. Ralfo kept throwing lanterns—he had a whole backpack of them too—and spat cow insults at me through gnashing teeth.

"Ralfo, shut up," yelled Sarah.

"I think Bernsy has a real gun," Grel said quietly.

Grel was right: the raging fire surrounding us shone off its polished surface, and I could see that it weighed down Bernsy's outstretched arm. I circled as I closed in on him until I neared the C sheep. My plan was to hurl my gun at the little gap just between Bernsy's black eyebrows and then dive behind the animal.

"Pin!" Grel and Sarah both yelled, and then Bernsy fired.

Maybe the sounds had come in the other order, but

it didn't matter. I was lying facedown beneath the sheep and blood swamped my buckskins. Grel and Sarah and Ralfo were all shouting, and on top of that, the tied-up wizards were screeching; the fire joined in sinisterly. I pulled the sheep's wool down over my ears and moaned, but it struggled back against me to raise itself up. I hauled with all my strength and heard Bernsy curse. The sheep was limp, I realized. It wasn't trying to get up; Bernsy was trying to drag it off of me. Bernsy must have shot the sheep just as I'd jumped behind it. The next time Bernsy pulled, I resisted for an instant and then let go and sprung up, knocking him to the ground. His gun clattered free of his grasp and I snatched it up, narrowly avoiding a lantern.

"Did you see that, Mr. Cormill?" Sarah yelled. "Ralfo's cheating by interfering with the duel."

"I've taken note."

I turned to look and, sure enough, Mr. Cormill was sitting on his suitcase by the fountain, his spellbook open in his lap, writing speedily.

"Pin!" cried Grel.

I jumped back just in time as Bernsy lunged at me.

"I don't want to shoot you," I said to him.

"I don't want you to either," he snarled.

"I'm a pacifist."

Bernsy didn't reply but advanced on me with raised fists.

"I'm going to shoot you in the foot. That seems pretty safe."

He swung at me, but without his previous enthusiasm. He was quivering.

"Do I just pull the trigger? Do I have to brace it against something? I've never done this before," I said, pointing it at his toes.

"I'd be happy to show you how it works!" Bernsy cried.

"Clever," I answered. "I'm glad to end it on that footing."

And with that, I shot him.

There was no escaping past Ralfo, who was big enough to fill the entire archway with his bulk, and every other direction ended in a wall of flames. Mr. Cormill still sat calmly, just out of reach of the flailing wizards.

"Pin," said Grel from behind his sheep. "This fountain leaks, too. Look! It runs off through a grate."

Grel pointed across the square. Beneath one of the streetlights was a rectangular drain. Sarah was already on her way to investigate it.

Bernsy was rolling around before me in agony, clutching his foot in both hands. His cloak had appeared black before, but now I could see it was a very dark purple velvet. I pocketed the gun, and with a clumsy swipe I cut a large swath of the cloak free with my hunting knife. Grel was looking on in horror, evidently convinced I was up to something very sadistic.

"I'm just getting some of this cloth for Squail," I explained, then ducked a lantern.

Bernsy was mumbling something.

"It'll mend, I'm sure," I told him.

Bernsy shook his head violently and let go of his foot to seize the front of my buckskin coat.

"Sarah!" he hissed emphatically into my face.

I fumbled the knife.

"Come again?"

"Your Sarah Beeley! She must've written the stupid manifesto under your stupid name!"

I was helplessly caught in Bernsy's adrenal grip. There was no hint of mischief in his wide eyes, but I didn't want them so close to my own. I wanted to be very far away so I could think.

"You're a fool, Charfo," Bernsy snarled, and then, at the sound of a crack, he fell back, limp.

Grel stood behind him, maneuvering the butt of my toy rifle in a sweeping follow-through.

"Let's get the hell out of here," he said.

Dodging lanterns, we zigzagged in the direction of the fountain.

"There are steps beneath this grate!" Sarah shouted to us.

I wanted to confront her about what Bernsy had just said, but Ralfo's vituperations kept me focused on the more basic task of preservation. With our combined strength, we were able to pry up the grate while the fountain and mass of screaming wizards still hid Ralfo from view. The water ran down the steps in a familiar way, and I looked up to see Grel grinning enthusiastically.

"Let's go, Ralfo's coming," Sarah urged, and we piled down into the darkness.

The steps were slick and we took them quickly, crashing down until we came to a landing. In the blackness, we felt around until our vision began to clear and forms took shape. We stood on the shore of a wide pool where a familiar sailboat was moored to a single bollard. Finally, I realized that it was very strange that we were able to see and wheeled around to find Mr. Cormill carefully descending the steps with an upheld lantern.

"Why didn't you help?" I asked.

"I didn't want to interfere with the evolution of the manifesto's story."

"Ralfo had no such compunction."

"Ralfo's approach is naturally quite different from my own."

Sarah and Grel were already in the boat, and Grel held the mooring line expectantly. Without another word, Mr. Cormill and I clambered aboard. Grel unfastened the rope and we slid off into the underground realm.

*

For a time, we all reclined silently. I avoided Sarah's eyes by looking up into the impenetrable gloom above. She had knowingly led me into the violence, which was uncharacteristically rash. I might easily have been shot or torched to death. And even before that, when Ralfo defamed me in my own column, Sarah hadn't so much as hinted at her involvement with the manifesto. A simple anger bobbed before my eyes, though I knew something more complex floated behind it. I tried to glimpse this notion, but the anger only coalesced and made me grind my teeth.

"I was going to tell you," Sarah finally said.

"Tell me what?" I answered, feigning ignorance.

"That I wrote the manifesto, Pin. I can see in your face that you figured it out somehow."

Grel didn't seem to be paying any attention. He was propped up on a wad of woolen blankets, mulling something over and lazily chewing on a cracker. Mr. Cormill was writing in his spellbook by the lantern light.

"But why?" I asked her. "Why would you do that?"

"Let me explain it to you now, because you should know." As she spoke, she anxiously wound her long hair around her index finger. "I wrote the manifesto, Pin, but it's such a horrid thing. You know how that happens, I'm sure. You sit down to write something, something you see so clearly in there with your thoughts, but it deforms as you scrape it out. It has its own agenda, its own impulse, and begins to look downward when you intend for it to strive upward. I dropped my pen when I'd finished—I really did, you can see the spot on my carpet. When I say *horrid*, I don't mean it's unskillful. I mean it's disgusting to consider. It's a manifesto that offers irresistible guidance but insists on you groveling in the filth for it. You can see what it makes of people. The manifesto sat on my table for ten days! I didn't want to touch it. But—I want to be honest—I'm a curious person, and a curious person can't have a loaded gun without eventually firing it. When I saw the result of publishing the piece, I knew right away that I'd created a monster in your name, but a mildly tame one with dull claws. I was pleased. It was enthralling. I knew you'd enjoy the mystery.

"Then the movement began to change unexpectedly. I observed that some other force beside the manifesto was at work on the members of the league. The collection of followers would be gathered in some place and would suddenly swell and cry out for no apparent reason. It was a confusing behavior and completely unexplained by the laws of the manifesto. Then, one day, I was idly watching a woman walking her dog through the park, and I saw the dog jump and howl in a manner uncannily like the action of my league. I soon learned that the dog had tread on a nail, and that was when I realized that my movement was under attack. Something was prodding my monster, and it was rearing back on its hind legs and honing its claws to fight back. Now that I knew what I was looking for, it didn't take me long to discover that Grel was waging a secret war on my adherents."

Grel perked up at the mention of his name and was now listening closely to Sarah's explanation. He fidgeted as if he impatiently wanted to say something but didn't want to interrupt.

"But this war had made them very dangerous, and although I was disappointed to, I felt it prudent to pin the whole manifesto on someone else. It didn't take long for me to decide on Bernsy. I know you've history with the fool, but I bet you don't know that I have some history with him, too. A year ago, I was reading by the river on one of those stone benches when I heard a cry and looked up to see Bernsy tussling with a young boy on the edge of the nearby bridge. As I watched, he overpowered the boy and pushed him headlong into the water. I bounded to the bank, because I saw clearly that the boy didn't know how to swim. Bernsy stood on the verge and trembled but didn't move to help. I shouted to Bernsy, 'Jump in and grab him!' He looked at me then, pointing down into the water, and said, in a steady voice, 'He will die.' I repeated my command, but Bernsy simply didn't move. I jumped into the river, of course, and soon I found myself clawing my way back onto the bank with the boy under my arm. Bernsy, still on his perch, swayed slightly but didn't say anything. I brought the child home and Bernsy evaded the police.

"Through a series of anonymous letters," she said, "I convinced Bernsy that he'd written the manifesto in his sleep and that you'd stolen the manuscript from his room. After this, things took a stranger turn—"

I stopped her there.

"Sarah, I know this will be an excellent story," I said. "I'll enjoy hearing about those anonymous letters, for sure."

"Of course."

"But you'll have to tell it to me later when I can listen to it with rejuvenated aesthetics. Before I sit back and stare off over this lake, just tell me why you published the manifesto under my name?"

"I published it under your name because . . ." She trailed off momentarily, looked at me coyly, and then quickly glanced away. "It was a flirt."

I felt my brow furrow.

Sarah turned her shining eyes toward me and fixed them on mine, her finger still mired in her hair. She was waiting for me to respond, but I didn't have anything to say. Her flirt had a charm to it, exactly the sort of charm I'd have chosen to be flirted with. And although she'd lost control of it all, in the end, I'd done rather well to defeat the consequences. I motioned for her to come to my side of the boat, and when she did, I took her hand.

I looked out over the water. Our light shown off the surface, creating a wide circle around the boat with only darkness beyond. We might have been riding a small sea on an unknown course through an unknowable abyss; we were floating on a lost sea.

There was nothing we could do to hasten our journey, so we entrenched ourselves in blanket nests and feasted on crackers until we became drowsy. We discussed inconsequential matters, and when we approached serious realms, we took Grel's tangents back to a safe distance until, finally, conversation faltered; I heard only Sarah's regular breathing in my ear. My mind wandered back to the lost sea. I wondered if there were fish floating along in it with us and photographs caught in its confused tides. If there were fish, did they eat crackers too? Imagining fish eating crackers led me to think about eating food without teeth, which led me to imagine sucking on candies. I would have liked to have a candy at that moment, I thought to myself. If I had one, I decided I would let it dissolve completely in my mouth. Why did anyone ever swallow candy? If the whole purpose of the thing was the taste, what purpose did it serve rolling around in your stomach? I sat up to propose the question to Grel but was cut off just as I started.

"Do you hear that sound of water?" Mr. Cormill asked, looking up from his writing.

We all roused ourselves and listened attentively. A faint trickling sound could be heard, distantly echoing from a source far beyond our boat's prow.

"It's the stream running down Mr. Selmare's steps!" Grel enthusiastically suggested.

"It could be someone in a different boat peeing over the side," I joked.

With his hand lazily resting on the tiller, Grel carried us toward the sound with the help of a soft breeze. We all listened in silence as the trickle slowly grew louder and more distinct. Soon, Mr. Cormill's lantern light shone off a distant object that steadily grew until it resolved into a wide stone wall punctured by a shadowed opening with a stairwell leading up through it and out of view. The foot of the stairs formed a narrow concrete dock with a single cleat fixed to a corner. A thin stream of water ran from the stairs and fell delicately into the lake.

That water sprang up from some dark reserve into the ripe lamplit air, then fell on the head of a wailing manifesto fanatic, spilled off onto an ancient plaza, and coursed back into darkness. Its brief visit hadn't given the water a chance to apprehend anything novel from the amazing things it experienced. It tumbled back down to join its kind, uncomprehending and disoriented, to stagnate for years until it was suddenly forced up into some other scene for a fleeting appearance. Someday, though, the water might not fall back down, but keep rising to join a cloud.

Or, it might be drunk by a bristled man wearing fingerless gloves, trying to snatch a moment of clarity before crashing back into the taproom. How disappointed that bristled man would be, for instead of fresh water he'd taste only photograph ink and the oily exudate of blind fish. And before his eyes, spots would form.

ABOUT THE AUTHOR

TOTE HUGHES LIVES IN GENEVA,
SWITZERLAND, WORKING AT
CERN IN PURSUIT OF A PHD IN
HIGH ENERGY PHYSICS.